Sink or Swim

Sink or Swim

Gerald Hammond

St. Martin's Press ⚏ New York

Library of Congress Cataloging-in-Publication Data

Hammond, Gerald.
    Sink or swim / Gerald Hammond.
      p.   cm.
    ISBN 0-312-15657-X (hardcover)
    1. Calder, Keith (Fictitious character)—Fiction.   2. Gunsmiths—
Scotland—Fiction.   3. Highlands (Scotland)—Fiction.   I. Title.
PR6058.A55456S54   1997
823'.914—dc21   97-798
                                                                        CIP

First published in Great Britain by Macmillan, an imprint of Macmillan General Books

First U.S. Edition: May 1997

10 9 8 7 6 5 4 3 2 1

ONE

I had had the shop to myself for most of the morning. Apart from occasional interruptions requiring me to dispense advice, lures or tickets for the association water, I had spent the morning on the firm's books.

The shop in the Square, Newton Lauder, I had proved to myself for the umpteenth time was only marginally profitable. Too many cowboys were offering cut-price postal bargains in this and that and especially in guns, cartridges and fishing tackle. It was the other, peripheral activities – gunfitting, repairs to guns and tackle, shotgun coaching, casting tuition, Keith's sideline in antique weaponry and my own dealings in vintage rods and reels that put the jam on our bread. On the other hand, we needed the shop to attract the customers, so the tail would have to continue wagging the dog.

Usually I enjoyed manning the shop, the serious discussions of fishing prospects and tactics, the occasional banter about blank days and the ones that got away and the exchange of money for goods which had been conceived for sport and refined far beyond mere utilitarian need. But today I was restless. Recent rain had brought the rivers up. The first really good run of salmon for more than a year had now begun and, although my lifelong love affair had been with the wild brown trout, I wanted to be on the salmon river,

1

enjoying the pull of the water, the spring of the rod and the occasional fight with a fresh-run fish.

My partner Keith, I knew, was where he should be – at home in his workshop, overhauling guns. He has been known to drop everything and slip away with a gun and a dog in pursuit of whatever quarry might be legal at that season, but I had found an excuse to phone him. Not only had he answered the phone in person but I could hear the hum of his small lathe in the background. That was all very well. The reassurance that he was pulling his weight had been offset by a request that I help him on the Sunday. The law, for some reason known only to itself, allowed no salmon fishing on the Sabbath, but I had hoped to go in pursuit of trout in certain small lochans that I knew, up beyond the high moor.

Our two wives had been off on some feminine ploy of their own, but when I took what must have been my hundredth look out across the Square at a perfect fishing day, warm but dull and with just enough breeze to ruffle the water, I saw Janet getting out of Keith's hatchback. Molly gave me a friendly wave and drove off.

Janet came into the shop and kissed the air several inches from my cheek. She is a natural blonde and whatever svelte means, she's it. 'Lunch will be on the table by the time you close the shop,' she said. 'You've heard the news?'

She would hardly be referring to the arrival of the salmon. 'Somebody came in for eighteen-pound monofilament,' I said cautiously. 'He'd heard that there was a drowning on one of the Castle Berry beats. Is that what you mean? He didn't know who it was.'

'Then I'm ahead with the news. It was Mr Berry himself. You know who I mean? Kenneth Berry?'

Out of respect we allowed time to pass in silence,

but it was only a fraction of a second. Ken Berry had not been anyone's favourite, not even mine despite his occasional custom at the shop. I have an irrational suspicion of anyone whose smile reveals an expanse of pink gum, and also a dislike of those who can't be trusted not to drag God into the conversation. 'I can't say that I'm greatly surprised,' I said. 'I presume that he was fishing at the time. He never wore a buoyancy aid or carried a wading staff, and when I told him that he might or might not live to regret it he suggested that I was only prophesying doom in the hope of screwing more money out of him. He had a habit of making offensive remarks.'

'But not a monopoly. Whereas, of course, you were going to make him a present of one of those new waistcoats,' Janet said. She slipped out of the door and I heard her feet on the stairs up to our flat.

I closed the shop on the stroke of one, locked up, took two paces to my right and climbed the stair next door. Above the shop was the flat that we had occupied for more than twenty years, ever since we were first married. It was small and we had intended to move as soon as family came along. But the family had never arrived and without any conscious decision being taken the flat had gradually been teased and furnished into fitting us. It was bright and airy, warm, comfortable and cheap. Half of what rent we did pay returned to us as half-owners of the shop. The view over the Square and the rooftops to the far hills was obscured for half the year by the ever-shifting panorama of treetops. Janet had chosen pastel colours and light, Scandinavian furniture to make the most of the available space.

There was soup on the table and Janet was setting out rolls, pâté, salad, fruit, coffee and a selection of cheeses. Lunch always took the form of a snack, but it was a good snack.

3

We sat and I continued the conversation where it had broken off. 'No, I wasn't going to make him a present of one of the new waistcoats,' I said. 'They cost the earth but they're the best thing yet. They have plenty of pockets, they inflate automatically if you fall in – but not for a shower of rain, which is clever – and they keep an unconscious man's face out of the water. What more can you ask for? They're a good buy.'

Janet was nodding. 'He was fishing, all right. They found his rod on the bank.' She returned to the more important topic. Janet has a good head for business. 'So if anybody mentions this or any other drowning, we point out that the deceased would still be alive if he'd been wearing one of those life-jacket waistcoats.' I was on the point of adding a few words when she said quickly, 'We point that out especially to the customer's wife. Right?'

'Ahead of me as usual,' I admitted.

Janet nodded, well satisfied. 'You've convinced me,' she said. 'I don't want to be a widow just yet. You've been known to fall in.'

'Twice in the last ten years,' I protested.

'Once would be too often if you happened to drown. Take one of them and mind you wear it.'

This was going rather too far. 'You know how much those things cost?'

'To the penny. It can be your next birthday present from me,' she retorted. That sounded very generous until I remembered where the money would have originated. Janet saw me hesitate. 'Give us an enormous discount,' she said. 'Keith's never slow to do himself a favour.'

She had reminded me of another grievance. 'Keith wants me to give him a hand on Sunday,' I said.

'On the shoot?'

'Where else?' We were referring to the family

4

shoot that Keith and I shared with Molly's brother and one or two close friends. It was a small and shoestring affair which had developed largely because several like-minded shopkeepers found it difficult to pursue their sport on a Saturday. It was sociable and fun and it was an easy way to entertain business acquaintances and return sporting invitations. I usually managed to slip quite a lot of the costs through before tax.

'Will you do it?' Janet asked.

'Not unless somebody lets me get away for a day's fishing beforehand,' I said. 'If I've minded the shop every day this week I'm going up to the trout-streams on Sunday.'

'I'll phone Molly and see if she'll split tomorrow with me,' Janet said. She tried to sound put-upon but I knew that she rather enjoyed queening it in the shop and startling the customers by showing far more expertise in the technicalities of shooting and fishing than her still rather glamorous appearance promised.

Relieved from duty by Janet and Molly, I had my day out. Sunday found me refreshed and willing to give up my usual day of rest in order to lend Keith a hand.

Along with the other tools specified by Keith, I put my .222 rifle into the car. I do not usually play much part in the keepering of our shoot – Keith and his brother-in-law are too expert to need much help from me – but having seen the havoc that foxes can wreak I like to do my share of control.

The outstanding work was mostly cutting rides through the gorse and brambles where the beating line of wives, girlfriends and relatives would usually grind to a halt or break up in disorder, but I went off on my own. The lack of three fingers on my right hand makes the handling of a chainsaw both difficult and dangerous for me. Keith and Ronnie between them could manage

5

the ride-cutting, while after our losses in the previous season it would be worth my while taking a scythe to cut back the grass and weeds around the feeding hoppers. If a visiting fox found it impossible to creep up unseen on the feeding birds, perhaps he would move on and creep up on somebody else's poults.

The first three feeders were in the shade of woodland and all that was needed was a trim of grass or nettles off the occasional hump. But the fourth was in heather. It was a clear case of the wrong tool for the job, but we had lost several birds in that vicinity in recent years. I slashed away with the scythe at the hard and springy stems until I had to give up, gasping. I promised myself that I would do a bit more on the way back.

The remaining feeders were in a grassy field. I walked the few yards, still breathing heavily. I had hardly started on the next when I realized that I was more tired than ever before in my life. I decided to take a rest from the scythe and walk along to look at the last two feeder positions.

I never got to the far end. The pain in my chest and left arm could have been put down to overdoing it with the scythe; but add dizziness, nausea, sweating, looseness and a feeling of total exhaustion and I knew that something had to be seriously wrong.

All the colour seemed to have gone out of the world. My body decided that it was not going to do more than lie down and close its eyes, but my brain was still working after a fashion. From far away I could hear the song of a chainsaw, but if I tried to short-cut through the woods and flaked out on the way I might not be found until some walking Gun stumbled on my skeleton. I would have to be my own rescue party.

With a great effort of will, I dragged myself upright and tottered unsteadily towards the cars. Several times I lay down in the mud, never quite sure that I would be able to get up again, but in the end the cars appeared in the distance and at last I was there. I collapsed into my own driving seat.

At least where I was I would be found, eventually. But that could be hours off, and what then? I closed my eyes and ran through several mental scenarios. Nonsensically, most of them seemed to end up with Janet searching the woods for our car at night while an impatient and possibly lecherous taxi-driver waited on the main road. I might have taken a chance on that, but I also remembered that my rifle was still in the car. The hassle with the police that would have resulted if it had been stolen was more than I dared contemplate.

I still don't know whether my decision was the right one. My doctor approves although the police would certainly not, but I drove nearly twenty miles to my local health centre through what I think is properly called a myocardial infarction. My left arm was almost useless but I developed a technique for changing gear with my right hand across my body. From Newton Lauder I was taken by ambulance and oxygen mask to Edinburgh.

The next two days I spent in the Cardiac Care Unit, hooked up to a monitor and also to a syringe-pump which was dribbling into my veins some preparation which they told me was designed to dissolve any blood clots still hanging around.

Janet, who shows the world an image of an independent and even uncaring woman, emerged in true colours. She followed me to Edinburgh (leaving, I am told, streaks of rubber on every bend), took a room at a nearby hotel and found her way unerringly to me through the labyrinthine hospital on about one visit in three, which for her was at least par for the course. She sat with me for many long hours, turning white and grasping my left hand convulsively whenever the trace

7

on the monitor, which was in clear view to both of us, skipped a beat. When it skipped two beats, her grip cut off the blood from my fingers. When it skipped at least three successive beats – after the third, who was counting? – I jerked my hand away before she could decide from the monitor that I was dead. I was already short of three fingers of my right hand so I preferred to keep the left intact.

After two days my pulse steadied and I was unhooked from the monitor and taken up to a ward. The medical insurance for which the partnership had been paying for many years would have entitled me to a private room, but the solitude of my cubicle in the Cardiac Care Unit had shown me that the price of privacy was boredom. The medical staff were adamant that stress must be avoided and I was soon in no doubt that boredom was stress.

Even so I might easily have been, once again, the Odd Man Out. All my life I have been plagued by a slight stammer. This nowadays only bothers me when meeting more than one stranger at a time. However, the first of the other five faces in the ward turned out to belong to Johnson Laing, a former pupil at my casting clinics, fellow member of one of the fishing associations, occasional fishing companion and regular patron of the shop, where he could be relied on to relieve us of any stock of rashly purchased, ingenious but impractical gadgets. On top of this, I had always rather liked him. Of the other four patients two were anglers, one of whom had suffered his own heart attack after hooking what was undoubtedly the biggest fish of his life – not, he pointed out, due to the strain of playing the fish but rather the psychological trauma when the hook broke. He admitted under questioning that the hook in question had not been bought in Newton Lauder.

The nursing staff were tyrants, one and all, but benevolent tyrants, dedicated to saving us from our own follies and in particular preventing the least physical effort by their patients. I was not, for instance, allowed to take the three paces to the toilet on my own feet but must ring for a nurse who would come with a wheelchair and solemnly wheel me to the cubicle in the corner of the room. To get the bath which by now I was desperately needing, I had to threaten to do a war dance around the corridors.

Visiting times were not as elastic as those downstairs in the CCU. Instead, the official hours were adhered to. So there was little to do except talk, usually of fishing; and with getting up strictly *verboten* we had to converse from bed to bed.

Janet arrived, considerably flustered, when the first visiting hour was more than half gone. I refused to be worried; as I guessed, she had found her way almost unerringly to the CCU, had been redirected and become hopelessly lost. She was, I noticed, wearing a fresh new outfit chosen for visiting the bedridden. She gave Johnson a nod and a half-smile, deciding that she knew his shopworn but humorous face from somewhere. She brought fruit, a magazine and some mail which had been carefully screened for anything provocative. 'Is there anything else you want?' she asked.

'Just to get home,' I said.

'You'll just have to be patient,' she explained.

'There's no point telling me to be patient,' I said glumly. 'You're really telling me to wait, which makes me about as im-bloody-patient as I can possibly get. If I were a patient sort of patient I wouldn't have had a heart attack in the first place.'

'Well, you'd better learn to be a patient sort of person without getting restive about it,' Janet said, 'because I've been reading the leaflets and you're going to have to do an awful lot of sitting around for some weeks.'

On that subject I had my own views. It never pays to start an argument with Janet before you have to. The ultimate outcome may be the same but the friction lasts longer. To change the subject I said, 'Johnson Laing was telling me some more about Ken Berry's death. I seem to have missed the papers while I was in the CCU.'

As a diversionary tactic it proved almost too successful. Janet, who had abstractedly been trying to identify Johnson's face by mentally placing him behind shop counters or in pubs, recognized the name instantly as having figured on a number of cheques to the shop and, to make amends, transferred herself to his bedside and went into her gracious lady act.

I got her back when visiting hour was almost over. 'He thinks he's going home in a day or two,' she said.

'He told me. We each think that. Sometimes it's true, as in my own case,' I said hopefully. 'He also told me that when Ken Berry drowned, Colonel McInsch tried to save him.'

'That's what it said in the papers,' Janet confirmed. 'He pulled him out and tried to resuscitate him.'

'I find that very strange.'

There was a murmur of agreement. The conversation was becoming general. 'I thought it was weird, myself, when I read about it,' said the rather *de luxe* young woman who was visiting the man in the far corner. 'Those two couldn't stand each other. They used to slang each other in the correspondence columns of the *Scotsman*.'

Janet nodded. 'But it's no use arguing with me,' she said. 'I wasn't there. I'm only going by what it said in the local rag – which will say anything to please a bigwig and has always been in the Colonel's pocket anyway.'

'Was anybody there?'

'The paper didn't mention anybody else. They printed a long interview with the ambulance driver. They didn't go so far as to say that there weren't any other witnesses – but that might have seemed a bit pointed, written about an unnatural death.'

As though the mention of death had brought her mind back to the reason for our being where we were, she began a lecture to me about staying calm, taking it easy, keeping my cool, not worrying about anything and above all not losing my rag. That lasted to the end of visiting hour and almost to the end of my temper. She then left, blowing a kiss in the general direction of Johnson Laing, before I could ask her to save me the press cuttings. She left behind her a slightly stunned silence. Not even the fiancée of the man in the bed in the far corner could match Janet's daunting femininity.

Keith showed up later. If I had tried to enter that ward after visiting hours I would have been thrown out on my ear, but not Keith. For one thing, he has the brass neck to carry it off. For another, although his salad days are far behind him and although he usually dresses on the assumption that before the day is out he will have dug the garden, changed a wheel or been invited to shoot or stalk, he has retained his looks and a courtly charm that was not lost on my favourite staff nurse, the red-headed one with the figure.

I don't know what it is that Keith has. I wish I had it. I might never use it, but I would like to know that it was there.

Keith brought with him a list of questions concerning the firm's bookkeeping and ordering systems – to which he would have known the answers if he had paid the least attention to me when I lectured him on those mundane topics. Janet would have gone for his throat, but I answered his questions without putting my arteries at risk. The fact that Keith this time seemed to be

11

making an effort to take in what I was saying, as if he knew that he might have to manage his own firm some day, made me wonder whether to feel mortal for the first time or to give thanks that some forward progress was being snatched from the jaws of disaster.

Business and the obligatory discussion of my prognosis dealt with, we got round to more general discussion. Keith, knowing that I would be interested in the circumstances of the drowning of an angler and client, had brought with him the cuttings about Kenneth Berry's death. It seemed that Colonel Ivor McInsch MP had been fishing on his own side of the river when he saw his neighbour slip and fall in. Hurrying downstream, he had managed to haul the other out onto a rocky outcrop.

'I can believe almost any of this,' I said as I skimmed through the cuttings, 'except for Ivor McInsch's attempts at life-saving.'

'And at resuscitation,' Keith said. 'You haven't got to that bit yet.'

I skipped several paragraphs. Mrs Waterhouse, the wife of the Colonel's keeper, had witnessed some of the action from her sitting-room window and had phoned for an ambulance only to find that a call had already been received. Such details as she could provide agreed with the shorter but more factual account given by the ambulance driver.

My reading skidded to a halt. 'The kiss of life?' I said disbelievingly. 'Mouth to mouth?' I tend to like my fellow men. Colonel McInsch, local MP, landowner and self-elected grand seigneur was an exception but he had ranked far ahead of Ken Berry. 'The reporter must be embroidering. Or else the Colonel's been doing a PR job on himself. They hated each other's guts,' I pointed out.

'No doubt of that,' Johnson Laing said. 'I heard the

two of them, about a year ago, each shouting that the other was a liar. This was on a garage forecourt in front of the pump attendant and half a dozen customers.'

'There you are!' I said. 'I can just imagine one of them fishing the other out of the river, to score Brownie points rather than out of goodwill, but mouth-to-mouth resuscitation? Never!'

'I wouldn't fancy it myself,' said the man in the far corner. 'Not to judge from his photo in the paper.' The cuttings had been passed from bed to bed and the photographs had not been flattering.

'I wouldn't kiss either of them for a bet,' Johnson said. 'But the same ambulance brought me in here. I was coming round a bit by then. It was still in the news and they were talking about it. They said that Colonel McInsch called for them on one of those yuppie portable phones he always carries, but even so they didn't get down to the river until about fifteen minutes after it happened and the driver said that the Colonel was still trying the kiss of life. And he was soaking wet to the eyebrows. He'd been in over the top of his chest waders.'

'Kiss of life be damned,' I said. 'He was probably sinking his fangs in Ken Berry's neck.'

'Not everybody is as unforgiving as you are,' Keith put in. 'Some of us would be prepared to let bygones be bygones, especially if we were fairly sure that the other had already fallen off the perch.'

'We'll see what the sheriff makes of it,' I said doubtfully. (There are no inquests in Scotland; if the procurator fiscal is unsatisfied, a Fatal Accident Enquiry is held in front of a sheriff.)

'The procurator fiscal brought it in front of the sheriff today,' Keith said. 'Accidental death. Ken Berry was fishing his own beat and he slipped and went in.'

'According to who?' I asked.

'I think the Colonel was the only witness called, but it'll be in tomorrow's local rag. He heard a yell, waded in and dragged the limp body out. I hear that the sheriff gave Ivor McInsch a pat on the back for his efforts and suggested that a Humane Society testimonial might be appropriate. Apparently you get a medal if you save a life but only a testimonial for trying.'

The meal trays arrived and Keith, his charm availing nothing, was driven out. He left me with some much-needed food for thought to while away the boredom of the long hospital nights. The Berrys and the McInsches stemmed from the same family roots and occupied a small castle and a fortified house which had been built within sight of each other for purposes of mutual defence.

According to local legend there had been a falling-out in Victorian times when a Berry had built a singularly hideous folly where it was hidden from Castle Berry by a fold in the ground but was in full view of McInsch House. The folly had long gone but the feud remained. A libel action near the turn of the century had nearly bankrupted both houses without settling anything, but both had survived. Unfortunately, both estates had sporting pretensions and it took only a game crop planted near the common boundary or a dog sent across it to retrieve a fallen bird for the smouldering embers to flame again.

The river formed part of the boundary between the estates. It was not a very important river, except to the riparian owners. Had it been more important it would also have been wider and deeper. As it was, it was at the hub of endless disputes. Some of these had arisen on the occasions when the river had changed its course.

Another lawsuit had later been brought to determine

the validity of the convention that one might properly cast from one's own side or even the middle of the river to the far bank, but that to wade to the middle and cast back towards one's own bank was in effect poaching. The court decided that the convention was good in law and thereafter recourse to the courts was avoided although not without some perilous feats of brinkmanship. The privilege of representing the constituency in Parliament usually belonged to the head of one household or the other except when by opposing each other they split the vote and let the opposition in.

My companions in the ward and several of our visitors would have discussed the tragedy endlessly; but by noon next day I had had enough reminders of death and was trying to forget that my lifespan was finite – and considerably more so than it had been a few days earlier. I remembered that the late Ken Berry's widow had never had any interest in fishing. The Castle Berry beats might be up for grabs. If I could rent them by the year and let them by the day or week, I could turn a nice profit as well as having some good fishing available for myself and friends. During her next visit I begged Janet to make enquiries, quickly before some other shark beat me to it. Rather than go herself, leaving me visitorless, Janet phoned Keith to delegate the task and Keith, in turn, passed the chore on to his wife, Molly. Back through the same channel came the reply. The fishing might or might not be put out to tender but it was not open for negotiation.

Five days after my coronary, Johnson Laing went home. On the same day, I was wheeled down into the basement and did eight minutes on the treadmill. The computer made warning noises whenever my heart stumbled, but the cardiologist seemed satisfied.

My favourite staff nurse interrupted Janet's next visit. She took us both into a side room, told us that I could go home on the Monday, showed us a video and read us a lecture about how to live for ever despite a dicky heart. The essence of it was to return to normal very slowly. First week home, stay in the house and don't climb stairs more than once a day. Second week, house and garden. And so on. When the video made it clear that sex was not to be considered permissible until at least six weeks had passed, Janet caught my eye and made a face. It occurred to me to wonder how old or infirm or inhibited had been the person who plucked that particular period out of the air. I saw the staff nurse watching us with amusement. She must have had a laugh a day from the reactions of the various couples to the precept.

Sunday, always the sort of day to get God a bad name, was even more of a drag than usual. The light at the end of the tunnel could have been the tail light of the train ahead.

Janet was to bring my clothes in on the Monday, but first the staff nurse haled me into the side room for a more than usually thorough check-up and an ECG. Conventions had eased greatly since the days of Florence Nightingale. The nurses were in summer uniform, thin white nylon which in some lights left little to the imagination, and the staff nurse was a well-built girl.

'How do you feel?' she asked suddenly. She was leaning over me at the time, her left nipple almost tickling my nose. Her question caught me unprepared. There was only one truthful answer and it nearly slipped out before I could stop myself. I made an inarticulate sound.

She could understand. It must have been an old story to her. 'No sex for six weeks,' she said. 'You know that.'

'Only five weeks now,' I pointed out.

'The six weeks start today. Sorry.'

Reminded of a grievance, I forgot to be embarrassed. 'That seems crazy,' I said. 'I never put into sex even one half of the energy that that damned cardiologist had me putting out on the treadmill.'

Her smile became a choked-off laugh. 'Thanks for the warning,' she said.

Twenty minutes later, Janet arrived with my clothes. I dressed, shook hands around the small ward and made my escape quickly before they could change their minds.

Janet, who on a shooting day could lug a bag containing a dozen rabbits with ease but on other occasions never expected to carry more than her handbag, insisted on humping my case, light though it was. That solicitude more than anything else brought home to me, as I emerged into the sunshine, that I was not quite the same person as I had been ten days earlier. Inside me, still beating after a fashion, was an organ I had never seen, never even bothered to visualize; but my continued existence depended on it. I had asked too much of it and in return it had given me a hell of a fright.

TWO

As if to reinforce that message, Janet drove us in our Audi. I was discouraged from driving for several weeks – not because of any danger of passing out at the wheel but because it is well known that drivers undergo stresses that pedestrians and passengers are spared. Neither of us was comfortable with the new arrangement. Our custom was that Janet only drove when I was either absent or had drink taken; it made her nervous to have me for a passenger in my own car while sober; meantime, I contemplated the verge rushing by much closer than usual and trod on imaginary brakes. By the time we pulled up in the Square at Newton Lauder, I think we were both beginning to feel that a second coronary would be less likely if I did the driving in future.

Things, I noticed, had been happening while Keith had undisputed control of the shop. My window display for the summer season, which had featured some quality fishing gear with a centrepiece comprising a salmon (stuffed), tastefully arranged on a square of dummy turf complete with fly (a Durham Ranger), one small rock, a net and the butt of a rod, had been swept away. In its place was a complete spectrum of shooting gear with, at its centre, my turf and rock supporting a gun (a cheap import), a game bag, a scattering of spent cartridges and a stuffed pheasant – the last apparently

18

still on its feet, which did not say much for the quality of the cartridges.

We would soon see about that, I told myself. But, in fact, my hope of taking command of the shop again perished stillborn. While Janet was helping me out of the car as tenderly as if I had been her rich and elderly uncle, Keith came out of the shop, hanging up the CLOSED sign (and on a weekday!) and locking the door behind him. At the same time Molly and their married daughter Deborah appeared out of nowhere. It was immediately clear that they were all much more worried about the state of my health than I was. They seemed quite prepared to link hands and carry me up the stairs, but I set off under my own steam and was shepherded up to the flat by all four of them, with a compulsory rest where a chair had been thoughtfully placed on the halfway landing.

One thing I was due to find out over the next few days was that, on top of the long list of things not to do which had been furnished by the hospital, many of my friends would combine to furnish a further list made up of whatever they had been doing when they had their first coronaries. Between the two lists, very few things were left that any sensible man would want to do – with the sole exception of universal medical advice that a drink or two would be permissible, if not highly beneficial, depending on the inclination of the speaker. With this weapon to hand I was able to persuade Janet to forget about tea with skimmed milk and get out the bottles. What could have been a sombre occasion soon became quite a jolly little party.

One theory, derived from no very certain source, held that red wine was the preferred drink for cardiac sufferers. Molly brought me a glass of Beaujolais from our slender store and sat down beside me. She and Deborah are dark and plumpish, managing to be very

19

attractive, in my opinion, without quite being beautiful.

'So Ken Berry's widow wouldn't play?' I said.

Molly made a face. 'Worse than that. I trailed all the way out to the castle and called as if I had come to pay my condolences – if that's the right expression. She was very gracious about it at first. She was on her own and seemed to be glad of a little company. But as soon as I mentioned the fishing she seemed to feel insulted that I'd dared to mention it.'

'Strange,' I said.

Molly shrugged. I saw a trace of the smile which she tried to hide whenever she was going to enjoy her own outspokenness. 'She always was a fool. I remember her when she was Dorothy Selkirk, the snob of snobs and never two ha'pence to rub together. Designer clothes from the Nearly New Shop and not a knicker to her name. I was going to make a polite exit when she suddenly accused me of coming on behalf of Colonel McInsch.'

'Why would she think that?'

'She didn't say. But thinking back, I remembered the big meeting the British Field Sports Society held two years ago. Keith spent half an hour talking to the Colonel about heather-burning while I stood nodding and smiling and wishing I could take my shoes off. The Berrys were there in the background, making snide remarks.'

As if she had reminded herself of the discomfort, Molly kicked off her shoes and tucked her feet up under her in that posture that no male can achieve. Not being very tall, she chooses shoes with heels too high for comfort. *Il faut souffrir pour être belle* . . .

'Anyway,' Molly resumed, 'the point is that she said I could tell the Colonel there was no way that he would get his hands on the fishing. She got quite hysterical and I couldn't make much sense of what she was saying, something about threats and not wanting trouble but she knew what she'd been told and if it came to making trouble her late husband could give as good as he got and she could pick up the something or other where he'd dropped it. Cudgel? Challenge? Banner? I don't remember.'

'Funny woman!' I said. 'Boiling it all down, in a nutshell we don't get the fishing?'

'That's another way of putting it. I tried to get it through to her that we had nothing to do with the Colonel but she couldn't seem even to consider the thought.'

Deborah came round with refills. I asked after her baby and the other subject was swept away on a tide of eulogy.

It soon became very clear to me that I was not going to be allowed to serve in the shop for several weeks in case an argument with a dissatisfied customer should cause me to clutch my chest and slump forward over the counter, to the detriment of our stock and customer relations. The general assumption seemed to be that, if not actually bedridden, I was to be wrapped in cotton wool indefinitely. On the other hand, due to the absences of Janet and myself for the past week, Keith had a backlog of gun repairs to overtake and he wanted Janet's help in the shop, whereas Janet wanted to brood over me like a mother hen.

With very little input from me, it was decided that Janet and Molly between them could manage the shop, referring any difficult questions to me over the phone and, as a concession, bringing me the paperwork at the end of each day.

'That should take care of a few minutes,' I said. 'What am I supposed to do for the rest of the time? Watch television?'

Nobody took that suggestion seriously. There was a

thoughtful silence. None of them had looked at it from my point of view until then.

'Rest,' Janet said at last. 'You're supposed to avoid stress.'

'Boredom is stress,' I said.

'He has a point,' said Keith. 'Write an angling book.'

'You have to be doing it to write about it.' I was beginning to sound grumpy, even to myself.

Deborah came up with the sensible answer. 'Do some fly-dressing,' she said, 'and write the definitive book. You always complain that commercial flies are overdressed. Mum can take the photographs.'

'Well—' I began doubtfully. With the stock of the shop to pick from, I had neither had the time nor any real need to dress my own flies for years.

'That's settled, then,' Janet said briskly. 'God knows I don't want scraps of fur and feather all over the carpet, but it's the least of the many possible evils.'

Before the party broke up, Janet had exhumed my fly-tying vice, tools and hoarded materials; Keith had descended to the shop and returned with a supply of hooks and synthetics and a selection of the furs and capes that I keep for special customers; and a table had been established for me in the sitting-room window. Later, Molly returned from a flying visit to her home. When pressed for time she sometimes froze birds in the feather and she had opened her freezer to pluck the tail feathers from several pheasants left over from the turn of the year. The tail feathers of the pheasant are the best single source of materials.

But I was not yet ready to resume anything as active as fly-dressing. Time in hospital had been so divorced from real life that I had had no standard against which to evaluate how I felt. But now, taking the first stumbling step towards normality, I noticed how easily I tired. The medication had to be to blame, because I had done no more that day than be a passenger in a car and chat with some old friends, but I slept away the afternoon and in the evening watched an hour or two of television with Janet before retiring to bed and sleeping again until morning.

Janet insisted on serving me my breakfast in bed, although I had had more than enough while in hospital of meals taken with my weight on my coccyx, a posture that I have always thought slightly less comfortable than the rack. Also, after a long, deep sleep in my own bed I felt fit for anything. My illness seemed to have become history like all previous illnesses, so it came as a shock to realize, once I was up and dressed, that Janet and others were still taking it very seriously and that I was not to be allowed downstairs on any excuse less than a major fire.

When I was seated fretfully at my table with my vice installed and my materials neatly boxed, Janet pronounced. 'I have to go out,' she said. 'Things have been piling up. Bank first, then around the shops to stock up for your low-cholesterol diet. Keith's downstairs in the shop. If you feel . . . anything coming over you, phone him straight away. He's going to phone you now and again, so if you have to go to the bathroom again take the cordless with you or you'll have him closing the shop and coming upstairs in a temper.' She stopped and studied me uncertainly. Evidently I was as new a person to her as I was to myself. 'I think that's all,' she said at last. 'Behave yourself.'

'Yes, Mother,' I said. She put out her tongue at me and left.

Years before, I had mastered the knack of tying flies. I had mastered it again with even greater determination after the accident that cost me three fingers of my right hand. But in the intervening years my remaining fingers

23

seemed to have lost their cunning. I fumbled around, mastering the knack for the third time, often unwinding my waxed thread and sometimes breaking it, just passing time, pausing to watch the real world go by in the Square below. Was this to be the story of my life from here on?

Word that I was home had been passed around. The phone sounded regularly as people rang to ask how I was doing. Some of the enquiries were mere gestures of politeness, but I was surprised to note how many people whom I would have put down as casual acquaintances sounded genuinely concerned. It seemed that I had more friends than I knew.

This telephone traffic, of course, tied up the phone until Keith came galloping upstairs, half expecting to find me, at best, unconscious with the phone in my hand. He was, as Janet had predicted, less than pleased.

There was one useful task that I could perform without offending against the laws of the Medes and Persians as laid down by Janet and others. I prepared our usual midday snack, and pressed the buttons on the microwave when I saw Janet coming across the Square. Janet seemed grateful for the small gesture. She had promised to do a turn in the shop that afternoon.

We had finished lunch and I was washing up while Janet rested her feet in preparation for a long afternoon on them when other feet were again heard on the stairs. Keith came in, carrying some sort of radio.

'I've been to see Jake Paterson at his electronics emporium. He was asking after you, by the way. He can't supply an intercom off the shelf.' Keith stooped and plugged the cord into a socket, leaving my lamp unplugged. 'Jake lent me two CB radios. We can't shut the shop every time we find your phone's engaged. These are set to what seems to be the least used channel. Just leave it switched on and receiving. Whoever's in the shop can ask you if you're still ticking. If you are, press this tit and you can answer – or, of course, to speak if you want something. In other words, if you need help, yelp. It has batteries, so you can unplug it and carry it around with you.'

He was gone again before I could say more than a couple of words. From the sitting-room window I saw him load several bagged guns into the boot of his hatchback. Either he was putting on a good act or I could assume that he genuinely intended to overhaul customers' guns in his workshop at home. I plugged my lamp in and left the CB radio to work off its batteries until Janet could bring me an adaptor.

My fingers were beginning to remember their old skills. I decided to tie a few elaborate salmon flies of the Doctor series before attempting the smaller and much more fiddly trout flies. But I was still being interrupted. I answered the phone to Janet.

'I'm all right,' I said. 'And it will be a lot cheaper if you use the radio while we have it.'

'There was some prat going "Breaker, Breaker!" on the channel. You must have heard. And Keith said not to use the radio for business calls,' Janet said primly. 'It's not allowed.' I knew that her real reason was that microphones, like cameras, made her mind go blank. The telephone, for some reason, had quite the opposite effect. 'I have a customer here who wants to know—'

While my eyes watched the folk scurrying around the Square, I answered a complicated enquiry about balanced combinations of rod and line as suiting the physique of the particular customer. It was soon clear that his present rod was too soft for him and I authorized Janet to give him a reasonable trade against a new one. We disconnected and I had peace for ten minutes during which I finished tying a Blue Doctor. It was not very evenly tied, but salmon are not as fussy as brown trout. I varnished the whip finish and set it aside anyway.

I was taking another envious look into the Square when the phone sounded its electronic note again. On the radio, a distant voice was seeking some very personal advice from someone who was, maddeningly, too far away to be heard as anything but an incomprehensible murmur. I turned the volume down.

The caller was Johnson Laing. 'How are you doing?' he asked.

'Bored out of my skull,' I said. 'I'm looking down into the Square, hoping that somebody will trip on the pavement or step in a dog-turd, just to bring a little excitement into my life. But no such luck!'

'That's how it goes,' he said. 'But life goes on.'

'If you can call it life.'

'We could liven it up a little. Do you want to come fishing next week? I have an invitation.'

'Trout, salmon or sea trout?' I asked him. Johnson had been let out of hospital before me but he still couldn't have been on the loose for as much as a week. I could just imagine either of us daring to cast one-handed with a light trout rod.

'Salmon,' he said.

'Next week? Literally next week?'

'Yes.' I thought that he sounded slightly defiant.

'You have to be out of your mind,' I told him. Casting with a fifteen-foot two-handed salmon rod, even a featherweight in carbon fibre, must put a considerable strain on the whole chest.

'Nobody said anything about fishing.' Johnson sounded as though I'd stolen his rattle.

I was on his side, but there were limits. 'They didn't say anything about bungee jumping either, probably because they didn't think anybody would be daft enough to try it. Anyway, you're not even supposed to leave your own garden yet.'

'I'm paying no heed to those claivers,' he said. 'And I'll be into my third week next week. Short walks allowed.'

'Not up to your arse in running water they're not,' I pointed out. 'I'm as keen as the next man and keener than most, but it seems to me that a little gentlemanly bank-fishing for trout might fall within the guidelines. Wading after salmon, no. You'd be dicing with death.'

'Suit yourself. But you'll miss the rest of the season if you stick to the letter of the leaflets. My doctor says my body will tell me what I can and can't do, and it's telling me not to pass up the chance.' He went on to make some comment about the prospects for an autumn run of salmon, but I could see a girl down in the Square whose short summer skirt was blowing in the wind, revealing a length of beautiful leg, and I stopped listening. I had already been celibate for a fortnight. Johnson recaptured my attention when he said, 'Have you heard the rumours?'

'What rumours?'

'You haven't, then. The word is that Colonel McInsch could have saved Ken Berry but decided not to bother.'

'That's hardly surprising,' I said. 'We've all been thinking it.'

'It won't do the Colonel much good when election time comes round again.'

'It's only the kind of malicious rumour that always gets bandied about,' I said. 'And it's impossible to prove or disprove.'

'It wouldn't have to be proved, not to the satisfaction of a court of law,' Johnson said. 'Better for him if it did. At least he could get a trial and be acquitted. But I don't think there's anything in Scots law requiring you to save a life. There is in America, I believe, but in this country, "Thou shalt not kill; but need'st not strive Officiously to keep alive".'

As it happened, I knew the quotation. 'The poet who

27

wrote that has been dead for more than a hundred years,' I said. 'Probably from salmon fishing. I wouldn't count on it still being good law.'

'Whatever the law says, public opinion will hang him.'

'Maybe,' I said. 'And maybe not. There will be those who would give him a landslide victory and carry him shoulder-high through the streets. The Colonel's PR man is probably spreading the rumours.' I was remembering more and more reasons for having disliked Mr Berry. As far as I knew he had not been evil on the grand scale, just nasty in a petty, back-stabbing sort of way and, in his churchgoing, a hypocrite. My various callers must have felt the same, because any creed of *de mortuis nil nisi bonum* had gone by the board.

Janet must have been trying to reach me on the phone, because as we disconnected her voice, audibly mistrustful of the medium, came faintly out of the CB radio. 'Are you all right?' she asked.

I put my hand out for the phone, then remembered, turned up the volume and fumbled for the SPEAK button on the CB radio. Before I found it, a man's voice came over the radio. 'I'm OK,' he said. He sounded surprised.

Janet must have accepted the voice for mine because the radio fell silent again.

Later on in the afternoon, Keith returned to the shop to keep an appointment with the traveller from a cartridge manufacturer. I would have liked to be present, because Keith is inclined to over-order and at today's interest rates stock lying idle loses more in value than is saved in quantity discounts, but Janet, relieved from the shop counter, arrived home and swore that if I went down those stairs I would find my chair on the landing and the flat door bolted in the unlikely event of my ever making it back. This lecture, I thought, and her refusal to be parted from me, were as much because Janet wanted to talk as for any concern over my health. She had been without her regular listener for most of every day for more than a week and she was showing withdrawal symptoms.

My medication was intended to slow down my metabolism. One side-effect was a strong desire for a nap in the afternoons. There had been no chance of a sleep while Janet was phoning every few minutes to reassure herself that I was still ticking, but I managed to doze surreptitiously while her voice receded into the background. She seemed to recall every visitor to the shop, which of them had asked after me and which of the gamekeepers had promised to save useful feathers and skins for me, and every word exchanged across the counter.

It was no more than a catnap; indeed, I think that I heard Janet's every word even if I did not bother to understand. When I began to take notice again I was sure that she had mentioned a name that had been in my mind. 'What was that about Ivor McInsch?' I asked.

'I said that I was sorry for him. Ever since he tried and failed to save Ken Berry's life – and there are thousands who wouldn't even have tried – there seems to be a whispering campaign against him.'

I yawned and rubbed my eyes. 'Saying that he could have saved Ken Berry if he'd wanted to?' I asked.

'They've been saying that for ages. Now they're saying that he told lies in court last year. It couldn't be true, could it?'

I remembered the case. 'It could very easily be true,' I said, 'and I wouldn't have blamed him in the least, but I expect it's just the usual malicious gossip. Don't repeat it to anybody or you may have to make a court appearance of your own. Any suggestion that he's committed perjury really would finish him in Parliament.'

'Three different people told me, so there must be something in it.' Janet spoke with such certainty that only later did her comment strike me as not only illogical but harking back to a much earlier system of justice. Or perhaps she was recalling Lewis Carroll and *The Hunting of the Snark* – 'What I tell you three times is true.'

Closing time arrived and Keith came upstairs from the shop with the day's takings and associated paperwork. As I suspected, he had over-ordered cartridges.

The restrictions placed on a heart patient seemed to be modelled roughly on the lines of the Ten Commandments with a great many *Thou shalt nots*. The only departure from the medical view that anything enjoyable had to be bad for one was the edict, already mentioned, that an occasional drink would do more good than harm. Keith, who is not usually a wine drinker, had brought a bottle of a decent whisky with him and we enjoyed a good dram apiece while we cashed up, did the books and wrote cheques to cover a couple of outstanding accounts.

Janet joined us while the fat-free evening meal was cooking. She was still curious about Colonel McInsch's rumoured misdeeds and soon managed to drag the conversation in that direction.

Keith seemed reluctant to commit himself, but in the end he said, 'I don't know whether McInsch could have saved Ken Berry. Personally, I'd have contented myself with throwing him something useful to hang onto, like a large rock. But I was always sure in my mind that he lied in court last year.'

'Same here,' I said.

Just then, Molly phoned up to ask when, if ever, Keith was coming home and at the same time the smoke detector went off because the toaster had once again failed to pop up. The subject of Colonel McInsch and his possible misdeeds got lost for the moment.

Although I was acutely conscious of the risk of precipitating another heart attack, or bringing on an angina which I had discovered to be almost equally unpleasant, I was just as wary of allowing my muscles to atrophy with disuse. As a compromise, I devised a system of exercises which could be performed without leaving the chair or attracting Janet's attention and which, I kept telling myself, when restricted to little-and-often made no extra demands on the heart.

It was Molly's turn in the shop next day. With Janet at home there was no need of the CB radio, but instead of turning it off altogether I used the opportunity to sample the other channels. On one, some clown who had ambitions to be a disc jockey was playing endless records of my least favourite sort of music. On others, drivers who were still enchanted with the radio as a new toy were solemnly telling each other where they were and what they were driving, with much use of the jargon of the medium. But among the dross were occasional scraps of almost philosophical discussion, emotional pleas, the making and breaking of dates and gems of humour. Once I was drawn into a conversation, offering hope to a boy whose father had suffered a heart attack.

Together with my view of the Square, this glimpse of the world outside helped me through the long boredom of waiting for my heart to progress towards recovery. I was surprised to find that I was not the laidback character that I had always thought myself to be. Perhaps this new impatience was the result of long years spent trying to keep up with Keith, whose nervous energy seemed to quiver in the air like microwaves long after he had gone.

Rather than dress endless copies of my favourite flies or those which might sell in the shop, I set myself to tie one fly in each common size of every pattern in normal use, from Alexandra to Zulu. This, I estimated, would run to a thousand or more trout flies, plus nymphs and lures, as well as the fewer but more elaborate flies for salmon and sea trout, and might well keep me occupied until long after the regime allowed me to go and try some of them on the water.

In mid-afternoon, Janet brought tea and joined me at my table. At the time, I was trying a Daddy-long-legs without losing track of events down in the Square, while at the same time keeping an ear open for anything interesting on the CB radio and systematically tensing and relaxing my various muscles in sequence. There is no better antidote to boredom than trying to do four things at the same time.

Janet frowned at the radio. 'Tell me about the court case Colonel McInsch was involved in,' she said.

I turned the radio down, let my muscles have a rest and looped my tying thread behind the rubber button to keep the tension on. Five simultaneous activities would be beyond even my capabilities. I took a biscuit. 'It was in the papers,' I said.

'But I'd no reason to pay it much attention. If we're talking about the same case, the Colonel wasn't involved in it. He was only a witness.'

'All right,' I said. I thought back. I knew what my conclusions had been but the reasons for them had faded. 'You know Colonel McInsch's keeper?'

'Jim Waterhouse? Of course I do,' she said indignantly. 'I've known him since I learned to walk.'

So perfect is Janet's air of urban sophistication that I sometimes forget that she was born on a farm, locally.

'About a year ago, he was prosecuted for poisoning birds of prey. Sparrowhawks, to be precise.'

Janet nodded energetically without disturbing one blonde hair. 'I remember that much, now that you remind me. I never believed it.'

'I didn't either. But why not?'

'Because, as I said, I've known him all my life. He's

compulsively honest. He believes so implicitly in the law that if the law told him to stand on his head before breakfast, he'd do it. And he's too good a keeper to use poisons. If sparrowhawks were taking his pheasant poults he'd find some legal way to keep them away. Or he'd buy some extra ex-laying hen pheasants to make up the numbers.' Janet paused in the act of refilling her cup and met my eye. 'Why didn't *you* believe it?'

I held out my cup while I thought it over. I was a fisherman with shooting as a second interest a long way behind, but Janet had been shooting with Keith and others for most of her post-pubescent life. 'I know him quite well,' I said. 'I agree that he's a very honest man. But that's only an impression and one can get it wrong – how else would any swindler survive? Also, of course, keepers do sometimes come to think of their poults as their personal babies and there's no denying that there are a hell of a lot of sparrowhawks around. On the other hand, I've been with Keith when he rubbed up against the two witnesses who accused Jim Waterhouse. I may say I wasn't impressed. They struck me as the type of absolute bigot who'll deny evidence that's staring them in the face if it doesn't agree with their pre-conceptions. They accused Keith of interfering with a badger sett and wouldn't listen to either of us in reply. They went so far as to suggest that Keith went in for badger baiting.

'One of them, Milne by name, Keith says is an active hunt saboteur and was one of the party that vandalized the game-bird research station at Cowriebog. The other, a Dennis Pratt, I already knew by reputation.'

'I know about him,' Janet said. 'He was pally with Ken Berry.'

'He's also a pillar of the more respectable agencies such as the RSPB, the SSPCA and the Green Party.'

'That should have lent weight to his words.'

33

'That was the problem,' I said. 'I've seen him talking downright twaddle on the box, but it was convincing twaddle unless you knew better – which the man in the street wouldn't even if the man in the farm-track did. He's one of those closed-minded, self-satisfied, pig-headed fools who are all for banning any activity other than their own. I kept my head down because apparently fishing was all right although shooting definitely wasn't. And if you can see the logic in that, I can't. Keith got quite hot under the collar about him and I could see the point. You'd think that any reasonable Green who wasn't a conscientious vegetarian would see the merits at least in pheasant shooting. Releasing birds into a carefully managed habitat, to live free-range and be recovered, if at all, months later or else to survive and breed in the wild, what could be greener than that?'

'Don't ask me,' Janet said. 'You're ranting to the converted. Watch your blood pressure.'

She was right. I took several deep breaths and resumed. 'The two of them seem to have hated keepers as a breed and were convinced that every keeper poisoned birds of prey as a matter of routine. Their hatred became focused on Jim Waterhouse and Jim's traps started disappearing. He caught them in the act and ordered them off the land. They tried to make a case that he was using illegal gin-traps but they were perfectly legal Fenn traps. That seemed to make them angrier than ever as if Jim had no right to put them in the wrong. Then, when they went on coming back, the Colonel took them to court and got an interdict forbidding them access to certain woods.

'That, of course, was the ultimate insult. And, by a strange coincidence, only a few months later they produced the corpse of a grouse chick well impregnated with alphachloralose plus the corpse of a sparrowhawk dead of the same brew.

'Jim Waterhouse was charged under the Wildlife and Countryside Act. When it came to court, nobody was quite happy with the two prosecution witnesses. There was only their word for it that they had seen Jim put down the poisoned bait near his release pen, but their stories agreed – almost too well – and it looked black for him. Then Colonel McInsch, and later his stepson, took the stand and they both swore that at the time of the alleged offence they had been fishing for salmon at Lady Pool – which could have been looked on as madly optimistic if anyone had cared to remember that the river was down almost to silt and that the salmon were waiting off the river mouth for a decent spate. Jim, they said, had been attending them as ghillie.'

Janet gave a silent whistle. 'I never knew the last bit and I'd forgotten the rest. So Colonel Ivor McInsch MP was lying his head off on oath?'

'That's my opinion and I'm not alone in it. Only the Colonel and his stepson know for sure.'

'And Jim Waterhouse.'

'Of course,' I said. 'But the sheriff preferred the word of a distinguished MP before that of two known fanatics and he made some caustic remarks about the credibility of the prosecution witnesses. Jim Waterhouse was acquitted, of course, and things got a bit nasty for the other two. Just what McInsch and his keeper would have done if there had been a move to prosecute the others for perjury I don't know. There was never enough evidence for that. The benefit of the doubt and the doctrine of being innocent until proven guilty worked for them just as it had for Jim. But I heard that it counted against both of them in their respective jobs.'

'If you ask me,' Janet said hotly, 'it served them right. They started the business of – what does the Bible call it? – bearing false witness and they left the Colonel with the choice of sticking with the truth and seeing

Jim go down the river for something he hadn't done or beating them at their own game. I don't disapprove, I'm just surprised that he had the ruthlessness to go through with it.'

'Any politician worth his salt,' I said, 'is quite prepared to say whatever the situation calls for, regardless of whether or not it happens to be the truth. And, what's more, he has to be a little nutty.'

'You think so?'

'Of course. Nobody goes into politics with the intention of staying on the backbenches and serving the public. Every damned one of them hopes to be prime minister some day. And you know what a thankless job that is. Everything he does has to be wrong. You'd have to be off your chump to want it – power at any price.

'Added to that, the Colonel chose, presumably of his own free will, to be a soldier. That meant that he had to be prepared to fight and possibly die for causes that he might not even agree with. Anybody choosing in succession the careers of soldier and politician has to be seriously off his trolley.'

Janet gathered up the tea-things. 'That's just because you're you and have different views and aspirations. You sit there,' she added, 'preparing to tell lies to all the poor little fish, and you call other people liars. I'm ashamed of you.'

When I opened my mouth to give a reasoned reply, she popped another biscuit into it and made a laughing escape. I had both hands occupied in the dressing of my Daddy-long-legs at the time. Tying knots in pheasant-tail fibres to make the legs requires more fingers than even a fully equipped person has.

A few minutes later, Keith phoned for Janet. He had to go and see a client. Could Janet come down and help Molly in the shop? Janet snapped a few questions at him, just to be sure that there really was a client rather than an invitation to shoot something, before agreeing.

I was left in peace. There had been periods in my life when I had wished that I could sit down peacefully and dress a few flies, but now that the wish had been granted I found that just as endless sunshine or a diet of strawberries must soon pall, undiluted repetition of even the pleasantest task brings a conviction that it would be even pleasanter to stop.

Outside the window was a mild summer's afternoon. I now felt that I could sympathize with Keith's occasional surrenders to temptation, when he would suddenly find some excuse to abandon the business and go off with a gun and a dog. I decided to postpone monotony by introducing some contrasts, jumping from huge salmon fly to tiny midge, from weighted nymph to dry mayfly.

The radio had been silent except for occasional monosyllabic exchanges between a man and a woman at a volume suggesting that they were close at hand, but I was jerked out of a daydream about my favourite trout-stream when a man's voice, perhaps the same man, said, 'They're shutting up shop. Over.'

'No sign of the writer?' asked the woman's voice. 'Over.'

'None. We'll jack it in for today.'

'Wait for me.'

It was too early for any shops to be shutting, but through the window I heard the clatter of the bank doors being closed, below me and some yards to my left. Seconds later a woman came out of the hotel across the Square and entered the back of a blue car that I had half-noticed parked nearby. The car drove off.

I went back to my fly-tying, but my mind was beginning to itch. Had the woman said 'writer' or 'rider'? I knew one writer who lived only a couple of miles away. The Gold-Ribbed Hare's Ear under my fingers was coming out crooked. I unwound it and began again.

There was another possible explanation. I reached for the phone and dialled the number of the local solicitor. For once, the dragon who protects him from any danger of having to do some work was caught napping. Mr Enterkin answered the phone himself.

His enquiries after my health I cut as short as I could without being rude. 'Something odd has happened,' I said. It took a minute or two to explain why I chanced to be listening to a CB radio. Then I recounted the brief exchange. 'The idea of somebody keeping watch on the bank didn't appeal to me,' I said. 'I was going to contact the police and risk making an idiot of myself if it turned out to be something perfectly innocent. Then it occurred to me that their accents were Scottish and seemed strong.'

'Telephones tend to exaggerate accents,' he pointed out.

'But it suggested that they might well be using Scots dialect and I remembered that lawyers are often referred to as "writers" in the Scots tongue.'

'Because my profession arose out of that of the scribe,' he said. 'Go on.'

'That's all. Can you think of any reason why somebody should be watching for you to show up at the bank?'

He was silent for some seconds, which was unusual enough in itself to make me sure of my ground. 'I'll call you back,' he said suddenly. The line died the death.

It was a full half-hour before he called me. 'Listen carefully,' he said, 'and please treat what I am about to say as confidential. Tomorrow morning at a given time – let's say eleven fifteen – I shall visit the bank. I would like you, if you will be so good, to watch the Square without yourself being obvious about it and at the same time to listen to your radio. Please arrange, insofar as you can, that nobody will be calling you up at that time. Is that possible?'

'More or less. Even if I'm alone here I can phone the shop a minute or two earlier. Then whoever's in the shop will know that I'm still all right. I can't guarantee that nobody else will call.'

'That seems reasonable. I shall visit you shortly thereafter and you can tell me what if anything you have observed.'

'With the greatest of pleasure,' I said. I find Mr Enterkin's style of speech is oddly infectious.

'I shall indeed be obliged. You may have difficulty in keeping our arrangement secret from your good lady. Instead, you might impress on her the need for confidentiality. I do not want word of this bruited about the town – or anywhere else.' He paused and I heard him clear his throat. His voice changed. Evidently he felt the need to finish on a more sociable note. 'Are you managing to keep yourself occupied during your convalescence? How are you passing the time?'

'Dressing flies, mostly,' I told him. There was silence on the line. He was probably composing a retort beginning. 'Ask a silly question . . .'

'Fly-tying,' I amended. To judge from the continued silence, that was little better. 'For the fishing,' I explained patiently.

'Oh, fishing!' he said, as though that explained everything.

THREE

Janet was at home next morning, so no call would come from the shop. I treated her to a careful explanation of what was expected of me. I would rather have delayed telling her about the ethereal voices and Mr Enterkin's strange requests, but there was a risk amounting to virtual certainty that she would demand my attention at a critical moment and refuse to surrender it without a lengthy explanation.

The day was bright and a hot sun beat in at me. I would have preferred to move my table or draw the curtains but I had to sit and sweat.

At eleven fifteen to the minute I saw Mr Enterkin emerge from the entry below his office. He vanished from my view, moving at his dignified pace in the direction of the bank. I had plugged my tape recorder in to the radio and I set it running.

'Here he comes,' said the man's voice.

Janet came bolting out of the kitchen. I felt my own surge of anticipation. We were onto something. A minute went by.

'He's at the counter,' said the woman's voice.

'Breaker, Breaker,' some moron said faintly in the distance. He was quite properly ignored.

The woman came in again. 'He's dealing with some papers.' Her voice rose. 'He's handing over a cheque.' There was a long pause. 'He was only making a deposit,' she said disgustedly. 'He's coming out. He's stopped at the cash machine but it's a small sum, two digits. Here he comes. Leave him be.'

I was leaning back, peeping round the edge of the curtain trying to be inconspicuous without looking unnatural. Janet came and leaned over me. 'Is Mr Enterkin coming to tell us what it's all about?'

'Be careful,' I warned her. 'Yes, he's probably coming, but more to gather information than to dispense it. You know how secretive he can be.'

'We're leaving,' the woman's voice said suddenly. 'Hang on.' The radio went dead.

A minute or two later, the same woman crossed to the same car and was driven away. She was carrying a light piece of hand-luggage.

'I've seen her somewhere before,' Janet said.

'She was trying to keep her face turned away,' I said.

'I've seen her, all the same. Or somebody very like her. I'll put coffee on.' She took the flat's front door off the latch and went into the kitchen.

That seemed to be that for the moment. I filled in a minute or two by varnishing the whipping of a Black Gnat and hooking it into a square of white foam plastic to dry, prior to transferring it to the board where my collection was beginning to take on a pattern.

The footsteps on the stairway were heavy but brisk. Mr Enterkin came in, very neat in his bowler with an umbrella in one hand and a rolled newspaper under the other arm. He was puffing, but very little considering his age and weight. He must have been nearly twice my age, his figure seemed to have been modelled on a rubber ball and he never willingly took exercise. Yet he stayed fit . . . and his heart remained sound. It was damned unfair, I decided, nodding to the chair opposite. He removed his bowler, revealing a round

41

and shining pate, and left his hat and umbrella on the side-table.

'Well?' he asked keenly.

I stopped the tape, wound it back and started it playing. Mr Enterkin listened intently to the terse exchanges. The radio itself began to mutter. The distant moron seemed to have found a buddy.

'If the lassie comes out, can I see her leave without myself being seen?' the solicitor enquired.

'She's already left.'

'That I would not have expected.' Mr Enterkin protruded his lips in deep thought and frowned at my board of flies. 'Not one of those would have fooled me for a moment. Not even if I were a particularly credulous and hungry fish. Tell me,' he said suddenly, 'could either of you have attracted the attention of a watcher?'

The kitchen enters off the sitting-room. Janet came to the door. 'I think I did,' she said. 'I'm sorry. Wal was lurking behind the curtain but when the radio said that you were coming out I looked to see if you were coming here. Does it matter?'

From the look on the solicitor's round face I could see that it mattered a lot, but he was too much of a gentleman to say so. 'I don't know whether it matters,' he said. 'If it means that there is no longer anybody waiting for an opportunity to mug me, then it may have been all to the good. Either way, it's in the past now. My boy, can you describe the protagonists? And the car?'

I could give him the make, model and colour of the car and had made a note of its number. 'I couldn't see clearly beyond the tinted glass,' I said, 'but I think that there were two men in the car. The woman was thirty-ish, slim, blonde—'

'About as natural as a silicon implant,' Janet said, popping out again.

'Yesterday, her face looked heavily made up,' I said. 'Her profile was sharp and she had prominent cheekbones but otherwise . . . I'd know her again, but there's nothing to describe. Today, she kept her face turned away.'

Janet came in with a tray of coffee and scones. Mr Enterkin began to struggle to his feet but Janet frustrated him by leaning across him to put down the tray. 'Surely you're going to tell us what this was about while you have your coffee?' she asked.

Mr Enterkin half settled. 'I only *think* that I know what it's about. If I'm wrong, you don't want to know. And if I'm right, it's confidential.'

Janet, pausing in the act of pouring coffee, looked ready to hit him with our best coffee pot. I caught her eye and winked. 'Quite right,' I said. 'You mustn't blab about your clients' business. We only engage you as our solicitor because we know you can keep a confidence. Anyway, we'll soon know what it's all about when the police come to take our statements.'

The solicitor sat back slowly and allowed Janet to force a cup of coffee on him. 'What on earth makes you think that it's a matter for the police?' he asked feebly.

'Somebody expected you to make a large withdrawal. The woman was watching from where she could see you at the counter. You walked into the trap, partly to have a look at the inside of it. Where was she? In a hotel bedroom?'

Mr Enterkin nodded reluctantly.

'The two men were waiting in a car outside the bank. You made sure that you could be seen to be carrying only a small sum of pocket-money.'

'Did I, now?'

'You did,' I said. 'And I can think of several possible explanations.'

43

'Can you, indeed?'

It was my turn to nod. For the first time since my heart attack, my brain was beginning to buzz. 'The first and most obvious is that those men were the police. They were keeping observation, hoping to catch you or your client making an illegal payment, possibly a bribe. Of course, the police don't normally use the CB wavelengths—'

Janet had caught up with me and I could see the light of mischief in her eye. 'They might use Citizens' Band if the bribe was going to a policeman,' she put in, 'as for instance to lose some evidence against a valued client. They wouldn't want him hearing messages over the police radio and realizing that he'd been rumbled.'

I had rather hoped that Mr Enterkin would be indignant enough to blurt out the truth but, although his eyes were popping and his plump face had turned as red as his favourite claret even to the top of his bald head, he was silent except for a small noise like a kettle coming to the boil. His lips were pinched tightly together, so the sound had to be escaping from his nose, or possibly his ears.

'But the police wouldn't have been waiting to pounce outside the bank,' I said. 'They'd have waited to close in when the bribe was being passed.'

I paused, waiting for a reaction. Mr Enterkin was frowning at the odds and ends on my table. He picked up my pill bottle. 'What's this?' he asked.

'Nitroglycerine,' I answered truthfully. He put the bottle down very gently.

'If it wasn't the police,' Janet said, 'some third party had got wind of the movement of a large sum of money and was waiting for a chance to hijack it.'

I saw from the solicitor's face that she had struck oil. 'And being forewarned,' I said, 'Ralph prudently made

44

sure that they could see that he didn't have it on him. No point getting clobbered due to a misapprehension.' I paused, but the solicitor was still in no hurry to speak. 'I think we can acquit him of passing bribes.' 'Too kind!' he growled.

'He has too stern a sense of duty for that,' I went on slowly, my reasoning only a few sentences ahead of my tongue. 'And from what was said, it was a large cash withdrawal they were expecting, not a cheque and not the collection of somebody's family jewels from the vault. So what,' I asked Janet, 'would induce a respectable family solicitor to make a large cash withdrawal from the bank and not want the police involved, even when it became clear that somebody had intended to rob him of it?'

'Kidnapping?' Janet suggested. 'Mr Enterkin was to deliver the ransom and the kidnappers were going to grab it without releasing the victim. Either the victim's already dead or they want a second bite at the cherry. Yes?'

That was one explanation which I hadn't thought of and it fitted all the known facts very neatly. I nearly went along with it, but Mr Enterkin's tense posture relaxed slightly and when he picked up his coffee I knew that it was a wrong track. 'Nobody's missing, that we know of. Try again.' I tried to look knowing, but in fact I had almost run out of ideas.

'I can't think.' All the same, she did think some more and leapfrogged clean over the idea forming in my mind. 'Got it!' she said at last. 'He's being blackmailed. Solicitors are notorious for straying off the straight and narrow. They get their clients' money mixed up with their own or borrow some of it for a speculation that goes wrong. Own up, Ralph.'

Mr Enterkin, whose complexion had been returning towards normal, coloured up again and his physical tension returned, betrayed by a jingle of the spoon in his saucer, but he said nothing.

I was ahead of Janet again. 'Not himself,' I said. Serious though the matter might well be, I was enjoying myself. For the first time since my heart attack, I was injecting a little sparkle into what was left of life. 'He's a garrulous old devil. This unusual but welcome silence can only mean one thing. It's a client who's being black-mailed. And so, of course, his lips are sealed.'

We waited expectantly but Mr Enterkin's lips were indeed sealed.

Janet and I have developed a knack of tuning in to each other's thoughts. 'Well,' she said, 'I think we should call the police. Mr Enterkin's hands are tied because of his duty to his client but if he was free to speak, his advice would be that whenever we have reason to believe that a crime is being committed it's our bounden duty to tell the police anything we know. Wouldn't it? Wouldn't it?' she repeated in Ralph Enterkin's direction.

The solicitor gobbled incoherently for a few seconds, but eventually he found his voice and his power of argument. 'I would never use such an archaic word as bounden, but in most circumstances my advice would be as you suggest. This, however, is a special case. I ask you to take my word for it.' He looked pleadingly from Janet to me and back again. We assumed our most supercilious expressions of disbelief. 'Very well,' he snapped. 'I know that you're only being mischievous, in order to twist my tail while at the same time indulging your outrageous curiosities, but mischief has toppled empires before now. I had thought better of you both, but this life is full of disappointments. Give me twenty-four hours and promise that you will speak to nobody about this within that time. I shall have to consult somebody with a view to deciding on a way

46

to convince you that your silence is imperative.'

I was tempted to send my compliments to that somebody by name, but decided that if my guess was wrong my present air of omniscience would be shattered. 'You have until this time tomorrow,' I said.

'Very well.' He rose, swatted at a fly on the table with his rolled-up *Times* and departed without ever realizing that the victim of his irritation had been my Black Gnat.

Keith phoned next morning, wanting Janet to take over the shop, but Janet, who was bound by my promise of discretion, found a variety of improbable excuses. Nothing, she told me privately, was going to get her out of the flat until she had witnessed Mr Enterkin's efforts to edge us away from the police. As the deadline approached, she put the percolator on to bubble.

Resolutely I got on with my fly-dressing, but pausing now and again for a glance down into the Square. The CB radio was silent except for some twit in a van on the main road, bleating for a friend. None of the cars in the Square was occupied by possible watchers.

I saw the solicitor leave his office, but the rendezvous must have been out of my sight. When two pairs of footsteps fell on the stair, they brought no surprises. Mr Enterkin was accompanied by Colonel Ivor McInsch MP. The Colonel looked to be more soldier than parliamentarian. He had silvery hair and a moustache very neatly trimmed, a face both lined and tanned and an upright carriage that made him look taller than his real height, which was already more than average. His manner was bland and unflappable. Being himself a fisherman he was immediately drawn, while the solicitor was still trying to introduce us, to my foam-covered board, which was beginning to fill out nicely. Instead of indulging in the usual vacuous conversational gambits, he used my magnifying glass to study the fresh-water shrimps which I had been reproducing in a variety of sizes, weights and colours.

He looked up into my face. 'I remember you now,' he said gruffly. 'You've been ill, I hear. Do you sell these?'

Janet brought the coffee. Mr Enterkin was again thwarted of his compulsion to make formal introductions because the gallant Colonel had pleasant memories of making purchases from her fair hands. If his moustache had been longer, he would undoubtedly have twirled it.

When at last we were all four seated at the same time and had been served with coffee and biscuits, Mr Enterkin called the meeting to order by the expedient of speaking loudly, drowning out a discussion which was mainly a monologue by the Colonel about water levels, catch-and-release and offshore netting.

'Colonel McInsch,' the solicitor said, 'has decided to take you at least partially into his confidence – rather against my advice, because a secret is no longer a secret as soon as one unnecessary person becomes privy to it. However, he feels that as well as being entitled to an explanation in return for the great service that you have already done for both of us you may even be able to be of further help.'

'I don't quite see how,' I said.

Like any good parliamentarian, the Colonel was perfectly able to speak for himself and he had had more than enough of Mr Enterkin putting words into his mouth. He took over the initiative by raising his own voice a notch above that of the solicitor, who fell silent.

'Of course you don't,' said the Colonel. 'Not yet. You did me a favour. You were bright enough to spot that somebody was planning a crime. If they'd pulled it off, I would have been out of pocket to a degree that I couldn't possibly afford and Enterkin might have been seriously injured. By warning Ralph Enterkin here you enabled us to avert it. It was unfortunate but no fault of yours that you caught the eye of the woman who was observing from the hotel bedroom and thereby gave them warning. Perhaps if we'd been more open at an earlier stage that little contretemps might have been averted.' The solicitor and the Colonel exchanged unfriendly glances. 'So we don't know who we're dealing with. That may not matter much. We have learned that the woman left the hotel without paying her bill and they may all have given up and gone home now that they suspect that they were being watched. What is more serious is that they were acting on information which may have come from somebody close to me. It is important to me that I find out whether somebody in my household tipped them off.'

I bit back what I had been about to say and waited. Some of the anomalies were beginning to make sense. The Colonel seemed to be disappointed at our failure to comment or to offer our help blindly. 'I'd like to tell you the whole story,' he said, 'but I think you'll see as I go along that my whole objective must be to keep the matter as private as possible.' Mr Enterkin, who had stiffened ready to intervene, relaxed, nodding to himself. 'In politics, one soon learns that it's impossible to draw a line and say, "Beyond this point nobody else must know." If a secret's going to be a secret, nobody knows it but those who already have it and in whose interest it is to keep it a secret.'

'That,' Mr Enterkin said to me, 'is pretty much how I expressed myself yesterday. Even I have not been entrusted with the underlying story, and,' he added with a trace of bitterness, 'I am under instructions not to ask.'

'That is absolutely correct,' said the Colonel firmly.

49

'So I'll just say that I was approached by a journalist, a freelance with connections to several of the tabloids. Hopped into the passenger seat of my car when I halted coming out of my own gates, would you believe? He claimed to have information, backed by the statements of two witnesses, which would be extremely damaging to me.' The Colonel flushed suddenly so that his hair and moustache looked whiter than ever. 'You'll appreciate that the least trace of scandal can ruin political ambitions. People in other walks of life can laugh off what will bring down a politician. In particular, think how many heads have rolled in recent years because their owners were caught out in a lie.'

The Colonel paused. I thought to myself of the number of politicians who had survived or recovered despite being unmasked; sometimes if corrupt, often if concupiscent, almost always if incompetent but very rarely if untruthful. Voters seem to appreciate veracity above all else, perhaps, I thought, because of its scarcity value.

Colonel McInsch picked up his story again. 'The journalist asked me for my comments. I told him that there wasn't a word of truth in his allegations and that if he published them I would sue. He said that a lawyer had already checked the material and advised that publication would be in the public interest and that there was adequate reason to believe that it was true. A libel suit would fail. So he said. He sounded convincing. I haven't been able to obtain a confirmatory opinion without revealing more than I care to.'

Mr Enterkin emitted a small sound by which he managed to signify that he was insulted. The Colonel ignored him.

'The witness statements, which he showed me, were only extracts and there was no clue as to who had made them, but some of the details were correct and verifiable and, all in all, they looked damning. The witnesses may have been lying or have made honest mistakes, either way I was sure that I was being set up. But if so, it was brilliantly done. So I asked him how much. He pretended to be shocked but hinted that his articles might be suppressed in exchange for a consideration. Not a political favour,' the Colonel added. 'He said that he could see no reason why he shouldn't sell the exclusive to whoever wanted to buy it. Hard cash, equivalent to the amount he could have earned from the tabloids for a juicy political scandal. And that, by his calculation, added up to real money. A very difficult calculation to verify,' the Colonel commented sourly.

'I decided that I was going to have to pay up, but only if it was going to be a one-off deal. I had no intention of providing him with a pension into his old age. I told him to contact my solicitor and I phoned Mr Enterkin here and asked him to guard my interests. He—'

The solicitor might occasionally be prepared to allow a client to speak for himself but he had no intention of allowing that client to usurp his own right to hold forth. 'I contacted the gentleman,' he said grimly. 'Negotiations took more than a little time. I required guarantees that the matter would be settled once and for all with no chance of a second helping. He, on the other hand, wished – still wishes – to receive the money free and clear with no risk of prosecution or violence. However, there was no great cause for haste. The money would be almost as valuable in a year's time, the allegations would be as potentially damaging, perhaps more so if certain cabinet changes in the wind come about. When we had reached agreement on a complicated but mutually satisfactory plan, I telephoned Colonel McInsch and advised him of the sum of money required, in cash, for final settlement.'

'And I,' said the Colonel, recapturing the initiative, 'told Mr Enterkin that I would make arrangements with the bank and then send him a cheque which he could convert into cash and hold in his office until arrangements for settlement could be finalized.'

'I have a very good safe,' the solicitor put in, 'which is also very well hidden. Nevertheless, I did not intend to draw out the money until the last possible moment.'

'And that seemed to be that,' said the Colonel, 'until you dropped your bombshell. There could be no doubt that somebody had got wind of the imminent movement of cash in the hands of Mr Enterkin, from which hands it would be relatively easily removed.'

'Unflattering but probably true,' said Mr Enterkin. 'Happily I was able to advise Colonel McInsch that my office had been empty apart from myself at the time of our salient telephone conversation and that I had kept no written record of our discussions. Such contingencies as a crossed line or phone-tapping being highly unlikely, it seemed that the secret must have leaked from McInsch House.'

'Or the journalist,' I suggested.

'I doubt it,' the solicitor said. 'Out of no more than instinctive caution I made no mention of the actual source of the hard cash but rather allowed him to believe that it would be collected in Edinburgh.'

For a moment, the Colonel looked smaller and older. 'As far as I know, only my stepson could have overheard that one crucial telephone conversation,' he said, 'or possibly the couple who have looked after me for more years than I could count. But I would prefer that blame fell on the daily woman or my occasional gardener.'

'Couldn't your telephone have been bugged?' Janet asked.

He smiled grimly. 'It happens, perhaps to politicians

more than to others. It wouldn't surprise me in the least if the security services monitored me from time to time. But this doesn't seem to carry their imprint. And if there was any such surveillance, the bug has been removed. I had the house swept by a firm of security consultants last night. However, there's no need to speculate for the moment. If we can identify these villains it should become clear who was behind them.'

'It still sounds like a job for the police,' I said. 'They could deal with the intent to rob without knowing the purpose of the target money.'

'No police,' the Colonel said in the voice of one accustomed to command. 'Their curiosity tends to stretch beyond the immediate purpose and they are notoriously prone to leaks.'

'That's true,' I said. Leaks from the police to the press had become commonplace in recent years.

'We're hoping that you can help,' Mr Enterkin said.

'Me?' I said incredulously. Until that moment I had considered myself to be an interested spectator. 'You must be joking.'

'Both of you. And this is no attempt at humour,' said the solicitor. 'Remember, this is for Colonel McInsch's peace of mind only. A little adjustment, discussions in circumstances where overhearing is impossible, a discreet arrangement to draw the cash through some other outlet and the agreement with the – ah – journalist can proceed in safety. It is even possible that the attempted hijack has already been abandoned.

'So, bearing in mind that a successful outcome is desirable but not essential, your qualifications are impeccable. Here you are, tied for the moment to your armchair overlooking the Square, so that you will observe if the lady should return.'

'Or the car,' said Janet.

'Alas, no. Surreptitious enquiries reveal that the car was stolen in Edinburgh a month ago. It was found abandoned this morning, with its registration numbers restored to the original, in the car park behind the police station. Most probably they have provided themselves with another by now – if indeed they intend to proceed with the attempted hijack.

'More importantly, in addition to sitting here, you are listening to your CB radio. If you could monitor it for us, you might pick up messages which would give us a clue as to who and how and what.'

'I could do that much, I suppose,' I said. 'But what if they've switched channels? I can't monitor all of them.'

'Why would they do that?' the Colonel asked. 'They don't know that they were overheard. And those who step outside the law usually do so because they're too lazy to make money within it.'

'You would not find either of us ungrateful,' said Mr Enterkin. I saw the gleam in his eye and guessed that he was about to get his revenge for being kept partially in the dark. 'In fact, from what Colonel McInsch was saying to me on the way here I would suppose that in return for this small favour he would be delighted to give you leave to fish his beats at any time. Isn't that so, Colonel?'

'Oh, certainly,' said Colonel McInsch. The words seemed to be dragged out of him. 'Perhaps not at any time, exactly. You'd better phone me.'

I avoided the solicitor's eye. 'How kind,' I said. 'How very kind!'

'He's not allowed to go fishing yet,' Janet said firmly. I thought that the Colonel looked relieved.

We repeated for his benefit the description of the woman that we had given Mr Enterkin, and our visitors departed. The Colonel had decided to buy a new salmon rod in the shop downstairs, he said, with an air of conferring a great favour. I suspected that that would be as far as his gratitude would stretch.

The morning had escaped, almost unnoticed. Janet threw onto the table the makings of one of our do-it-yourself snack lunches. These had been a feature of our life throughout our marriage and, even though butter was now taboo, egg was usually omitted from the pâté sandwiches and there was only low-fat cheese to go with the oatcakes and honey, I still found them both filling and comfortably familiar. The addition of a glass of red wine, strictly for medicinal purposes, made up for any deficiency.

'What did you make of that?' Janet asked with her mouth full.

'Much the same as you did,' I said. 'And not quite what the Colonel was trying to imply.'

Janet nodded her sleek blonde head. 'Not by a mile,' she said. 'He has the politician's knack of saying a lot without telling you anything.'

'I wouldn't go as far as that. He hinted at the politicians' habit of trying to lie their way out of trouble and ending up much deeper in the muck than ever. He followed it up by saying no more than he had to, so avoiding any need to lie.'

'Unless his protestation of innocence was itself a lie. There's a lot of money involved,' Janet pointed out. 'There must be, or a gang of not less than three baddies wouldn't be investing time in it. Not to mention the cut they may be giving their informant. I don't see the Colonel parting with quite so much of his worldly goods to cover up an allegation of a tarradiddle.'

'He might,' I said, 'if it was his own tarradiddle and not somebody else's. Quite apart from the power and prestige, which some people seem to find a turn-on, there's a lot of money in climbing high up the political ladder and only a pittance in staying at the bottom. He was quite right in what he said. In nine out of ten political storms the incompetence, immorality or downright dishonesty might have been forgiven, but Parliament doesn't like being lied to. And the general public is quite sure that it's being lied to all the time, so it kicks up hell when it gets proof. If Nixon after Watergate had said, "All right, it's true, but everybody does it, so what?" he'd have ridden it out.'

'You think Colonel McInsch lied to Parliament?'

'Or an oath before the sheriff,' I said. 'That would be worse. Perjury,' I explained.

'Ken Berry's death? Or the alibi for Jim Waterhouse?'

'Either. Or both. We're guessing. He may have committed some heinous sin about which we know damn-all. But Berry's death would make sense. Imagine the Colonel fishing his own bit of water. Somewhere upstream there's a splash and moments later his neighbour floats down, waving his arms and crying, "Save me, save me!" or words to that effect. What does the Colonel do?'

'I can't speak for the Colonel,' Janet said thoughtfully. 'For myself, remembering the way the late Mr Berry used to eye me up and down I'd probably give him a cheery wave in return and go back to my fishing.'

'Very likely,' I said. 'I would probably have done the same and so, it's reasonable to suppose, would the Colonel. Up to that point he would probably still be on the right side of the law. And most of those who have fallen foul of Ken Berry would sympathize. But most of the population, and even some of the local voters, have never even heard of the man. So the Colonel goes in front of the sheriff and testifies, on oath, that he did everything possible to attempt a rescue.'

56

We had finished eating and Janet was gathering the used plates, but she stopped. 'And then?'

'And then, let's suppose that he is approached by somebody who has witnesses, maybe even a videotape, of the unfortunate Mr Berry drifting downstream, waving his arms—'

'And the gallant Colonel, local hero and Member of Parliament, waves and shouts back, uttering some old service expression such as, "Save yourself, Buster, I'm on dry land." If that got into the media, he could be had up for perjury and, on top, lose a whole lot of votes.'

Janet pushed the dishes aside and sat down again. Her face was serious. 'So what do we do? Mr Enterkin would tell us, as he's probably told himself, that we don't know anything and so the Colonel has the right to be presumed innocent.'

'More to the point,' I said, 'we haven't been asked to take any action to do with the drowning, nor in direct connection with attempted blackmail. We've been asked to help because there was a plot to rob Ralph Enterkin, presumably with threats or actual violence.'

Janet thought it over and then nodded. 'Don't just sit there,' she said. 'Switch on the radio.'

FOUR

The weekend passed and a new week made a welcome arrival – welcome because it brought some slight relaxation of the regime.

I was now supposed to have the freedom of the house and garden. I pointed out that the garden, which Janet kept in order, was of little interest except as a drying-green; but surely the shop, which in effect formed the ground floor of our house, was now within bounds. Janet was doubtful of the stairs, but when a crisis arrived over manning the shop she gave in and I spent much of the Monday behind the counter, doing good business and very much enjoying human contact while still managing to listen to the CB radio.

Unfortunately, that evening I suffered an attack of angina. Janet blamed the stress of serving in the shop while I preferred to put it down to having been cajoled into doing the washing-up. Either way, I was relegated to my fly-tying again.

It seemed that traffic on the CB radio was going to remain for ever limited to inane greetings between strangers and the passing of information which nobody with any sense could possibly want to know. Occasionally cryptic snatches of conversation could be made out, but if coded messages were also being passed I was unable to recognize them. Whenever the original channel was being monopolized by some obviously innocent chatterboxes I sampled the others, but I knew that my chances of happening on a significant exchange were negligible. Over dinner on the Tuesday, we agreed that the ungodly, whoever they may have been, had probably realized that their target was wise to them and had gone to lay siege to somebody else.

Only the next day we proved ourselves wrong.

Keith, peevishly protesting, was on shop duty again. Janet was at the public library, undertaking the thankless task of changing my books for me. And I was in my usual chair, bored out of my mind. Fly-dressing in moderate doses I find therapeutic, but I was beginning to dream about endlessly tying flies which then took wing. I was looking out of the window at a perfect day, warm but with a breeze to cool the skin or to ruffle the surface of water. The sun was too bright for satisfactory fly fishing. Fish, having no eyelids, are easily dazzled. This was fine by me. If I was to be kept away from the rivers, why should anybody else be free to enjoy perfect conditions?

I saw Janet on the far side of the Square, hurrying with her head down. She went into the phone-box, and a few seconds later the phone at my elbow made peeping noises. I lifted it.

'Wal?' Janet's voice said. 'Don't say anything, just listen – there's only about tuppence left on my phone-card. The blonde bimbo's sitting in a red car further along the road, where she can see the shopfront, but she's out of your sight and she can't see me here.' There was a brief pause while Janet audibly drew a long breath. 'A man got out of the same car and he's in the shop now, talking to Keith. She gave him some money. He's big with black hair and a fawn golf-jacket. Try to—'

Her card must have run out at that point because there was a click and the dialling tone came on. But that did not matter. I knew exactly what to try to do. I had seen the man approach the shop although his face, which he had not tried to hide, had meant nothing to me.

I phoned the shop number and Keith answered. 'When your customer leaves,' I said, 'try to get him to turn his head.'

Although Mr Enterkin was continuing secretive, Keith knew that something was up because the solicitor had prevailed on Molly (who was and is a successful amateur wildlife photographer) to lend me a good camera with a suitably long-focus lens. 'That'll be quite all right, sir,' he said.

I readied the camera and arranged the curtains to hide me without spoiling my field of view.

The man left a few minutes later. He seemed to have no hesitation about showing his face, but he cut diagonally across the Square, which only enabled me to get a couple of shots of his left ear and the back of his head. Then Keith came into plain view and I heard his voice. 'Did you drop this, sir?' he called. He was holding up an envelope. The man looked round and through the reflex viewfinder I saw that he had beetling brows and a boxer's nose but a small, soft-looking mouth. An easy face to remember and to describe. He hesitated and then shook his head and walked on.

Janet gave him time to get clear before leaving the phone-box and crossing the Square. It was some minutes before I heard her key in the door and I guessed that she was paying a call on Keith.

'He bought a priest from the shop,' she said as she entered at last.

'He probably needed a cosh,' I said.

'Maybe. But Keith says that there were cheaper and heavier ones. He bought one of those good brass and stag-horn priests and he said that an angler friend had a birthday next week.'

I shook my head. 'It doesn't ring true. No hard man would risk coming back here for the sake of a friend's birthday.'

'Probably not,' Janet said. 'But the woman would. She handed over money, remember. If she had a boyfriend who'd mentioned wanting one, she'd move heaven and earth. She couldn't come here herself, knowing that we'd seen her face, so she sent in an associate who's never been seen here except in a car with tinted windows. We'd never have suspected him if I hadn't seen her in profile as I came out of the library. I had to hurry right round the back of the old kirk to get to the phone-box.'

'Can you describe the car?'

'A small red Fiat. The number plates looked slightly home-made.' But she gave me the number anyway.

I phoned Mr Enterkin and passed along the information. 'I probably have a passable photo, if you want it,' I said. 'Shall I get the film developed?'

'Put it aside,' he said after a pause. 'If you don't hear from me again today, you can take it that no further action is needed.'

Janet had been listening on the bedroom extension. She rejoined me with her eyebrows soaring. 'After all that fuss and bother . . .' she said.

'Colonel McInsch only wanted to know who in his immediate circle was passing information,' I pointed out. 'Ralph Enterkin must have reason to believe that one of them, and it's not difficult to guess which, goes fishing and has a birthday to come.'

'That makes a lot of sense,' Janet said.

That evening she stooped to look over my shoulder. 'All this mention of birthdays reminds me. What would you like for yours?'

61

'I thought you were going to give me a buoyancy waistcoat.'

'You can give that to yourself,' she said, 'if you really think you're going to go on fishing. I don't want you to go down thump.'

The thought that I might not fish again had never occurred to me. 'I'm in absolutely no doubt about it,' I said.

She looked at me doubtfully and then decided not to press the point just yet. 'What else do you want?'

'To get out of here,' I said glumly. 'I'm bored stupid.'

'Is that what's doing it?' She laughed and kissed my ear, then settled in the chair opposite, showing some very pretty leg. 'You're too modest – you're not stupid, only mildly daft. Have patience. I want you to live for ever. Don't make me hide your clothes, or something.' She was quite capable of it, too.

'According to the book of rules, I could start going out and about on Monday. I'd settle for your promise not to be difficult about that.'

She looked at me again, more anxiously than I had ever seen her. 'We'll have to see what progress you make,' she said. 'I don't want to be pinned down just yet.'

Her choice of words brought another thought into my mind. 'I would rather like you to be pinned down,' I said. 'As long as I was doing the pinning.'

'Is that at the bottom of the depression that's been eating at you?'

'I'm beginning to feel that nothing worth living for will ever happen again, that I'm just waiting for death.'

'But that's not right,' she said uncomfortably. 'It isn't like that at all any more. I know heaps of people who had their first heart attack ten, fifteen years ago. They don't play rugby or run in marathons, but you were never one of the hearty types anyway. They live carefully active lives. You just have to ease back into it.'

We weren't quite on the same wavelength. 'I'll try to explain,' I said. I was explaining as much to myself as to her. 'I've spent most of my life looking forward, working for the next thing to come. Now I don't know what's ahead. I can only look back. And behind me, most of what I see—' I broke off. I was going to say that I could see nothing behind me but regrets, but I was afraid that my voice would break. I had been warned that I might find myself to be more emotional than ever before and it was becoming true.

Janet met my eye and looked away quickly. 'Tell me,' she asked, 'do I make your heart beat faster?'

'Always,' I said, equally lightly.

'I talked it over with Alice Morton. Her husband was a doctor until his coronary. He reckoned that the raised heartbeat from sexual excitement came within the bounds of calculated risk.'

'I don't quite see—' I began.

Janet turned pink. 'If you could be quite passive . . .' she said breathlessly.

'Oh, I could.'

That night, our relationship progressed into a new and beautiful phase.

No ill effects followed our lovemaking. Janet accepted that the doctors seemed to have got the medication right and the embargo wrong and she made no objection when I began to take gentle exercise around the town. Nobody argued about my doing half-days in the shop, either, or wandering over to the hotel for a glass of the house red. On my first jaunt across the Square, enjoying the sunshine and the fresh breeze and feeling rather like a traveller returning unexpectedly across the Styx, I found Mr Enterkin sipping a dry sherry at the bar. Over my glass of red wine I challenged him to deny that the combination of a birthday and the purchase of some fishing equipment had told the Colonel all that he wanted to know. I could tell from the way that he shushed me that I was near to the mark.

More to change the subject than from any need to know, he asked, 'You're continuing to make strides towards a full recovery?'

'Strides are out but, as I assured you not more than five minutes ago, I'm plodding in that general direction. And while we're talking about the Colonel—'

'But we aren't,' he said quickly.

'Yes we are.' But I took pity on him and turned away from the subject of blackmail. 'Did he mean his invitation to fish his water?'

Ralph Enterkin looked past my left ear. 'Should you be fishing yet?'

'Maybe not. But I'm supposed to avoid stress. They forget that boredom is stress.'

'At last you strike a chord with me,' he said. 'If the Colonel wasn't sincere he certainly should have been, after the efforts you made on his behalf.' He met my eye. 'Perhaps I did rather force his hand. And we wouldn't want him turning resentful, as is the regrettable habit of those who are indebted to others. Leave it until I've spoken to him again. I'll let you know.'

'Thanks. Tell him that that's my price for becoming incurious.'

We parted. I was threading my way towards the door through the assembled drinkers when I bumped into Johnson Laing. His placid face and mild eyes were unchanged but in baggy corduroys and a loose sweater he looked almost as untidy as he had in hospital pyjamas, in contrast to his usual dapper state. He insisted on stumping up for another drink apiece and we compared notes. We were about neck and neck in the recovery stakes.

64

Along with the drinks Johnson bought himself a small cigar. 'You're still smoking, then?' I said coldly. I had stopped about two years previously. Smoking has no opponent to match the reformed smoker.

'No, I've stopped,' he said. He brandished the cigar. 'This? Neither here nor there. I'd kill for a puff of my pipe. The trouble is that it would probably kill me. But I can take a cigar and not bother if I don't see another one for days. So it's stopped being a habit and become just an indulgence.'

'When do they let you back to work?' I asked him.

'Not for weeks and weeks,' he said cheerfully. 'And weeks. The powers that be quite understand that taking a class of determined malcontents would probably kill anyone in my delicate state of health. Anyway, they'll be breaking up for the summer before the end of the month. I still plan to get in a little trout fishing even if I never did manage that trip to the salmon. Fancy joining me?'

'I fancy it very much.'

'How about tomorrow?'

'I was thinking of a fortnight's time,' I said. 'We're not supposed to be exerting ourselves yet. The physical effort of casting—'

'Plus all the mad excitement of it all. I know. I tried my salmon rod on the lawn the other day and I have to admit that it did put a strain on the chest. So I was only thinking of a little trouting,' Johnson said. 'There's no great physical effort in strolling along the bank and flicking a dry fly into the ring where a fish has risen.'

That was different. 'I'm on,' I said. 'But who would drive us?'

'I'd drive us, if need be,' he said defiantly. 'Yes, *I know*, we're not supposed to drive until the six weeks is up, but that's not because we might flake out at the wheel, it's in case of the stress if we have an accident or a breakdown. If you feel strongly about it, I'll get

65

my niece to come and chauffeur us. And I'll even bring lunch. How about it?'

I remembered that Johnson lived several miles outside the town. 'You have your car with you?' I asked him.

He misunderstood me and bridled. 'My niece brought me in. Anything wrong with that?'

'Nothing at all. Let's go and see if I can smuggle a rod and a pair of waders out of the flat and into your boot while Janet's busy in the shop.'

'Fine. I'll catch you up in a minute.'

When he came out of the hotel he was lighting another small cigar.

Janet, who was addicted to shopping although she pretended to find it the ultimate bore, was heading off on a shopping trip and so was defensive rather than curious as to where I was off to, only wishing to be assured that I was going with a friend, that the friend was male, that I had my Nitrolingual spray in my pocket, that my friend knew how to use the spray, that somebody else was driving and that I was not going to overexert myself. I assured her that I was getting a lift into the country and only intended to go for a short stroll, omitting to mention the possibility of playing a fish while up to my waist in water.

Johnson's niece was waiting, as instructed, some yards off, roughly where the blonde woman had parked a few days earlier. This, I decided, was just as well. The niece, Heather, was an attractively chubby brunette in her early twenties and not the sort of company with whom Janet would have appreciated seeing me drive off, even chaperoned by the lady's uncle. I joined Johnson on the back seat of his estate car, in case Janet should be looking out as we passed by.

'Where are we going?' I asked as we moved off.

'We thought we'd leave that to you,' Johnson said uneasily. 'You know all the waters.'

So I was expected to stretch one of my carefully hoarded invitations to include Johnson. I was tempted to direct our course towards one of the more expensive day-ticket waters but, when I came to consider, what was being asked of me was a small enough return for the provision of lunch, transport and an incentive to get out of my chair and live again.

The fine weather was holding. I could think of one place where the bright sunlight might not spoil our fishing. 'All right,' I said. 'Carry on as far as the main road and turn left.'

Heather, it transpired, was married to an oil industry technician who worked two weeks offshore and spent the next two at home. Because they were not long married, their fortnights together were very precious to them, so Heather had given up her job and would be available to drive us around for two weeks out of the three which remained before we could legitimately take the wheel.

Ten miles to the south of Newton Lauder we took to a side-road and left it for a track which climbed over a spread of moor where sudden rocks poked palely out of heather. The road descended again into a valley. Trees overhung a broad stream which in places ran deep and in others was laughing and gurgling over a gravel bed. The landowner was an avid collector of unusual weaponry and gave me access to his treasured fishing as a sort of retainer for keeping a lookout, through Keith, for the items still missing from his collection.

We parked where the track petered out in a small beech wood where birds sang. Johnson's niece collected together a small pile of magazines and a rug. Johnson and I threaded up our gear, smeared ourselves with insect repellent, donned waders and set off. The woodland was too heavily undergrown for casting from the bank to be practicable. Johnson waded upstream from the car while I walked down the bank ready to wade up again.

There was no steady rise, but insects were falling or being blown from the trees and trout were feeding, sometimes deep but sometimes snatching a fallen insect from the surface. There was very little room below or between the branches for a back-cast and I yearned for my shorter brook rod. It made for varied interesting fishing, with a fresh challenge every few yards.

By twelve thirty, I had three trout of nearly a pound each and had returned several of their smaller brethren to the water. I had fished my way almost back to the car. The unaccustomed exercise and fresh air had given me an appetite.

Johnson, with one fish in the bag, had joined his niece and was already tackling the sandwiches. They had set up a picnic on a grassy rise set back from the water and the trees. In Scotland in summer trees can mean midges and the midges had already found areas which my insect repellent had missed. The combination of sunshine and a breeze was midge-free and comfortable.

We chatted as we ate, first about the fishing. Johnson wanted to know why I regularly outscored him. I gave him a few flies identical to those I was using. 'All things being equal,' I said, 'if you don't match me with those, you're probably missing a lot of takes. You're casting well enough.' Then, when that subject seemed to be exhausted, it seemed polite to draw Heather into the conversation. For lack of any better topic, I asked her how she had met her husband.

She smiled at an amusing memory. 'I was out with another boyfriend and he introduced us,' she said.

'They had been students together, years before, and we happened to bump into him in a club in Edinburgh. Tommy took a fancy to me and phoned me up a few days later. Nick was hopping mad.'

'Nick Lamontine, was that?' Johnson asked with his mouth full. 'I remember that you went round with him for almost a year. He's some relative of Colonel McInsch,' he added to me. 'Nephew or something.'

'Stepson,' Heather said. 'I was still going with Nick when his mother, the Colonel's wife, popped off. The Colonel wasn't a bad old stick before that. Since then, he's built a sort of crust around himself. It's funny that Nick's name should come up,' she said, 'because I saw him yesterday for the first time in about a year. I bumped into him in the Square, coming out of the hotel. He asked me whether we could do with a paying guest.'

'He must still fancy you,' Johnson said lightly.

She gave the idea serious consideration, while absently trying to pull her short skirt down over her knees, and then nodded. 'I think he must, because he's been living at McInsch House for years. Actually, we could do with a lodger but I didn't tell him that. He's one of those very intense men, brooding and virile, who get an idea in their heads and never get it out again. I . . . just wouldn't want to be alone in the house with him.'

There could be other reasons than lust for Nick Lamontine being on the lookout for digs – for instance if the Colonel had booted him out. 'He fishes, doesn't he?' I asked.

'He's very keen,' Heather said. I seemed to have set her conversational ball rolling again. 'I think that that's all that keeps him here, because he and the Colonel were never more than polite to each other while his mother was alive. Oddly enough, her death seemed to draw them together. And, of course, I suppose that he would have been rent-free at McInsch House as well as having free fishing. He doesn't have to stay at any particular place. He writes rather creepy novels and magazine stories, supernatural mostly, and they can't pay very well because he's always short of money. And, of course, he's very extravagant.'

'Which,' Johnson said, 'would have made him a desirable boyfriend but a very bad husband.'

Heather accepted the comment as perfectly reasonable. 'That's another reason I wouldn't want him as a lodger. I'd never have been paid, or not without being made to feel that I was taking the bread out of some other creditor's mouth.'

'Somebody was in the shop the other day,' I said, 'buying some tackle as a present for somebody's birthday. Does he have a birthday about now?'

Heather keyed up the date on her digital watch. 'That's right,' she said. 'In fact, it was yesterday. His birthday came exactly a month after mine, which made it very easy to remember. That's the only reason I was sorry to break up with him. Tommy has a birthday in the middle of nothing and I'm always in danger of forgetting it, except that he starts dropping hints several months before it arrives.'

I went back to the water with Johnson and watched him for a few minutes. He was on top of the problem of casting in confined conditions but he was not keeping his eyes on the floating part of his line so that he was probably missing a lot of takes. I tried to show him how to cast upstream and stay in touch with his fly without inducing an unnatural drag. I waded in to demonstrate and on my second cast the fly was taken with a force that almost broke my line. I thought that I was into a salmon until a spotted monster came out of the water and danced on its tail for a full second.

70

'Sea trout,' we said with one voice.

Until that moment, I had still been weighed down by the feeling that life as I had known it was over. The enforced inactivity, along with the effects of my medication, had reduced me to a state that I had not known since my youth, a state in which I was content to drift along, savouring or enduring the moment without wondering where it might lead. But no, the viewpoint was not the same. In my childhood I had been waiting for life to begin. This was different.

In an instant, everything changed. A sea trout on trout gear is a challenge to any man. If I could land this one, I would know that life was not over, while if I 'went down thump!' (or more probably 'splash!') my life would at least end on a high note instead of a long, low groan.

The fly the fish had taken was on a four-pound leader. Nylon line can usually take more than the nominal strength, but knots or old kinks can weaken it. I dared not keep up a high tension nor allow the fish a chance to jerk except against the soft springiness of my light rod. On the other hand, I must not let him reach anywhere that he could snag me in weed or rocks or round a sunken branch. It was a delicate walking of a tightrope – yet at the same time stumbling in water over slippery stones. Upstream we went, with Johnson cursing and splashing behind.

As luck would have it, the place where the fish had snatched at my fly was clear of snags, but not very far upstream was a half-sunken tree surrounded by the debris that had drifted down on it. I would have to turn the fish before he reached that perfect sanctuary. I applied as much pressure as I dared and held my tackle together by will-power.

It was only when I found that my left arm was becoming useless that I recognized the angina brought on by effort and excitement. To go on was crazy. I could be throwing away my life. I could have handed over to Johnson, but he did not have the experience for what was a very tricky task. Instead, I had him come and squirt his own Nitrolingual spray into my mouth. When I remembered to think about it, the pain had receded. It was a triumph of matter over mind.

It took me twenty minutes to bring a sea trout of no more than six pounds to the bank where Johnson waited with the net. It was a beautiful fish, bright silver with brilliant spots. No record breaker as sea trout go but he had put up a good fight. He would have been delicious poached and even better smoked, but Janet would have exploded if I had let her know of the escapade and, besides, I had been fishing for brown trout and to have a sea trout take the small fly in broad daylight – sea trout more often move and feed by night – and then stay on the hook was no more than a fluke. The lactic acid induced in his blood by the long struggle might yet kill him, but he deserved the chance to breed which had brought him back up from the sea to the water that had nursed him. Moreover, he had done me a bigger favour than all my friends put together. We unhooked him and I held him upright in the stream, rocking him so that water washed through his gills, until he made a sudden kick and was away. I wished him luck.

We collapsed on the bank, Johnson and I. I used my spray for a repeat dose and I noticed him making surreptitious use of his own. Adrenalin is not good medicine for a heart condition. I thought that we had probably been in more danger than the fish. Johnson's doctor had said that his body would tell him what he could and could not do. But Johnson's doctor was wrong. All that my body told me was that I shouldn't have done it. But I knew that I would do it again.

That was more than enough fishing for one day.

When our heartbeats had steadied and the breathlessness had passed, we walked slowly back to where Heather was deep in her magazines. There was still some tea in the flask and a half-bottle of whisky in the basket. To fish for more brown trout would have been an anticlimax after that sea trout.

'Finished?' Heather asked. 'How many more in the bag?'

'None,' Johnson said. 'But that isn't the point. You can't measure enjoyment by the size of the bag.'

'I saw you dashing around down there,' Heather said sternly. 'You're a pair of old fools. Just don't have another attack, either of you. I couldn't carry you and I'm sure the other one shouldn't.' She turned a page of her magazine. 'But if it'll help you to die happy, who am I to try and stop you?'

There was no answer to what was obviously a rhetorical question.

When we had refreshed ourselves, we packed our gear and our catch into the estate car and persuaded Heather that any more fresh air would be ruinous to her complexion. We swayed and bounced carefully along the track to where it met the tarmac side-road. Here, Heather had to pause to let another car, a Rover, go by from the direction of the main road. I had no more than a glimpse of the occupants as it passed, but the driver's window was down and the woman glanced in our direction. It was the blonde woman who had been spying on Ralph Enterkin. There were no individual features to which I could have pointed as proof of identity, yet there was no mistaking the combination of a sharp profile with straw-coloured hair cut in the then fashionable pudding-basin style. The man beside her was no more than a blur but he could have been the man whose photographs I had taken as he crossed the Square.

'Follow that car,' I said to Heather.

'Why?' she asked. I should have expected it.

'Please,' I said. 'Don't waste time. I want to see where they go. And don't get too close. They mustn't know that we're following.'

My last few words were a waste of breath. The Rover had been travelling dangerously fast for the narrow country roads and it was already beyond the next bend. The Renault was more manoeuvrable for the tight corners, but it was also heavily loaded for its power. We saw the Rover ahead of us several times but lost sight of it when the countryside became more wooded. When after a few miles we came to a T-junction there was nothing whatever to tell us which way it had turned, nor was there a soul or a human habitation in sight.

I sighed. 'Let's go home,' I said.

Heather used the T-junction to turn the car. 'What was all that about?' she asked.

I had had time to think up an answer. 'I spotted somebody who owes the shop money,' I said. 'We don't have an address for him.'

'If we see the same car again, shall I block the road?'

'Definitely not,' I said.

FIVE

Janet had always had a bossy streak. Hers was a benevolent dictatorship and I refused to resent it or the occasional remarks of male friends who speculated aloud as to who wore the trousers in our marriage. Perhaps my friends were right. Rather than live a life of contention, I had fallen into the habit of pretending to accept Janet's every edict and then doing my own thing. On the rare occasions when she noticed what I had done, remembered what she had said and felt inclined to make an issue of it, I would nod and smile and agree with every word of her remonstrations, which disarmed her and usually ended in a gale of laughter.

Since my heart attack, her determination to make my decisions for me had redoubled; and when I walked in with my parcel of trout the danger flags flew immediately. But I explained quite honestly that I had been chauffeured both ways, had caught them without stress and felt much the better and more relaxed for my outing. It seemed simpler not to mention the sea trout. Janet was sufficiently pacified to be easily distracted by the news that the Colonel's stepson seemed to have been given his marching orders and that I had had a fresh sighting of the blonde woman. She had ushered me firmly into my usual chair and now she took a seat for herself.

'Are you going to tell Ian?' Ian is Keith's son-in-law, a policeman and head of the low-powered CID presence in Newton Lauder.

'I don't know,' I said.

Janet set her jaw. 'I won't have you being harassed and getting called as a witness and having to attend identification parades and things. As far as Mr Enterkin's concerned, the matter seems to be closed. If he can let it drop, so can we.'

'But,' I said equally firmly, 'if the gang had given up, they'd have left the district. Those must surely have been a couple of hard men who had been brought in to chase after a particular sum of money and split the take. The lady may have been an intermediary or a paid-up member of the firm. I've heard at least one short message passing on the CB radio which could be a discreet pair of lovers but could have been them again. If the woman's still here I think the men are still around, so it seems likely that they may still be hanging around in the hope of a crack at the money.'

'It's possible,' Janet said reluctantly. Another slant occurred to her. 'And while they're waiting, they won't want to stop earning. Unless young Mr Lamontine is subsidizing them – and it doesn't seem as if he's got the money – they may be pulling off other robberies.'

'There have been several crimes between here and Edinburgh, according to the papers,' I said. My status as an invalid had given me time to digest the newspapers more thoroughly than ever before. 'I think I should at least warn Mr Enterkin.'

'That would be the same as telling the cops.' Janet got up and fetched our collection of large-scale maps of the locality on which we were in the habit of recording information about the ownership and boundaries of farms and rivers. I pointed out where we had first seen the Rover and where we had lost sight of it. 'It may

76

not have been the same woman,' she said. 'And if it was, she may have stayed around because she's Nick Lamontine's girlfriend. And she may have been driving out there for a one-off visit and for some quite other reason. You didn't recognize the man at all?'

'I barely saw him,' I said. 'It could have been the man I photographed in the Square. It could just as easily have been Lamontine himself.'

'We'll drive up there tomorrow,' she said, studying the map. 'Whichever road the Rover took, it couldn't have gone very far after the T-junction – both ways peter out in a mile or two. If we can get a sniff of the men, we'll tell Ian and I can make all the statements. Otherwise, I'll find some way of letting Mr Enterkin know that the woman's still around without involving you, and he can make of it what he likes.'

I had made a tentative arrangement with Johnson for another fishing trip on the morrow, but it was probably better to postpone it. Two days running might have provoked an adverse reaction from Janet – or from my damaged ticker.

As it happened, both trips had to be postponed. Keith's daughter, Deborah, managed to put her husband's car through a dry-stone wall and into a field, breaking her wrist in the process, which engaged the attentions of both Keith and Molly for the next day – more to mind the baby and defend Deborah from her husband's wrath than to cosset their injured but guilty daughter. Keith had been due to drive to Edinburgh to fetch a collection of antique handguns which had been bought back from the executors of a late client's estate; Janet, as a partner in the shop, was covered by the dealer's licence and agreed to make the journey in Keith's car (provided only that Molly combined her baby-sitting with monitoring my well-being over the CB radio) rather than allow me to face the stress of driving in the city. So I had the shop to myself for the day.

Between customers, I used the time to straighten out the paperwork, which Keith had once more managed to transform into a midden, and make a start on fresh VAT returns. In mid-afternoon, I was replacing a dull stack of cartridge boxes in the window with a colourful display of my new salmon flies when Jim Waterhouse, Colonel McInsch's keeper, walked into the shop.

I had been acquainted with Jim for nearly twenty years. He was a lean man with a good head of silver hair and a ready smile. A few years previously I had gone, with a borrowed dog, to help him out when his pickers-up had let him down on the day of an important shoot. The day had passed without disaster and after the bag had been disposed in the game room and the other chores had been attended to we had adjourned to a nearby pub. There, battle had broken out between rival groups of football supporters. The landlord had been unable to cope, so, having by then put a few drams under our belts, Jim and I managed to subdue the principal troublemakers and to imprison them in separate cubicles of the ladies' lavatory until the police arrived. These things form a bond. Since that day, each of us had counted the other a friend. I had never told Janet of the incident.

Jim had heard of my indisposition. While I was still in the CCU I had had a conventional get-well card signed by him but more probably emanating from Mrs Waterhouse. He brought me a selection of *cul-de-canard* – literally 'duck's bum' – feathers which he had saved for some visitor to the estate who would now have to manage without them. He shook my hand very gently, as though afraid that a more violent greeting might be more than my health could bear, and asked me how I was going on.

'I'm well on the mend,' I assured him. 'It's just a

matter of getting the medication right, making haste slowly and not doing anything too daft.'

'Aye. It'll be a while before we can take on the lager louts again. Or before you're back at the fishing.'

'I hooked and landed some good trout yesterday,' I said proudly. He whistled. I could have mentioned the sea trout but the less said about that the better. Janet knew Jim's wife well and the Colonel's view about secrets was undoubtedly the correct one.

I booked Jim's order of cartridges for the coming season and sold him some snares. His eye was caught by a game carrier and he added that to his purchases.

'You'll not be allowed a drink, I'm thinking,' Jim said.

'Wrong again,' I told him. 'A drink is the one indulgence I'm left with. Alcohol dilates the blood vessels or lubricates the platelets or something else highly technical.' I glanced at the clock. 'The bar will be open in about twenty minutes. Hang on a while and I'll shut the shop early.'

'Yon Keith doesn't mind?'

'He does it oftener than I do. We just put a note on the door saying where we can be found, in case a client turns up with an urgent need. It's a good system. Anybody fetching me out of the cocktail bar feels obliged to offer me a drink.'

'I'm fetching you into the bar,' Jim said. 'Does it work the other way round?'

'Dream on,' I told him.

Jim took the shop's only chair, reserved for our better clients, and waited patiently while I finished my odds and ends of work. I used the CB radio to advise Molly that for the foreseeable future I would be in reliable company and signed off. Interrupted only by a pair of late customers quickly dealt with, we kept up a disjointed conversation.

A card of silent dog-whistles reminded Jim of something. 'You maybe won't believe this,' he said. 'At the tail-end of last season, I met up with a man I kenned. He had a wild-looking young Labrador at heel. Trained it hisself, he said. I asked him was the dog any good. "Damn fine dog," he says. "Retrieves to hand every time. And he doesn't hang about waiting to be told what to do. He's away for the retrieve while the bird's still falling." Would you believe, it was minutes before I realized he'd found a way to tell me the dog was a chronic runner-in and still make it sound good?'

For the good of my heart I checked myself from laughing as heartily as I might have done. I was developing a restrained chuckle which put the minimum of vibration through my chest. 'That sounds like a politician's dog,' I said.

'You're close. It was Mr Berry. The late Mr Berry. You heard about his death?'

It seemed that Ken Berry's demise was never to be out of my thoughts. And I was still curious enough or bored enough to fish for more information. 'I was in hospital around the time,' I said. 'I saw what was in the papers but I never heard the details. I wouldn't have thought that you were on speaking terms.'

Jim tapped his nose and looked smug. 'A keeper canno' aye join in his boss's feuds. I'd no great fondness for Mr Berry, mind, but he sought my help from time to time, having neither keeper nor ghillie of his own, and he was a braw tipper when he was pleased.'

'But it was a real feud?'

'Real enough. I never knew the Colonel to swear, except when Mr Berry's name was mentioned. So don't you go telling him what I just telled you.'

'I wouldn't do that,' I said. 'Were you there?'

He shook his silvery head, almost regretfully. 'Nobody was there,' he said. 'Except the Colonel, that is. Edna saw the most of it from the sitting-room window but she's not one to interfere. I was up on Hollin Hill, the wrong side of the crest, among the trees, topping up the pheasants' feeders. The first I knew was seeing the blue light on the ambulance turning off the main road. I thought maybe something had happened to Edna or that the Colonel had had another heart attack.'

The words caught my attention. 'He's had one before, has he?'

'Seven or eight years ago. Slowed him down for a while but you'd never know it now.'

'I'll be damned.' I felt suddenly optimistic. If the Colonel could be so spry and active, at his age and seven or eight years after a heart attack, perhaps I had a future to look forward to after all.

Jim had resumed his tale. 'I hurried over the hill,' he said, 'wondering what was adae, and got there just as they was lifting the stretcher inside. So I ken little more than yourself.'

'Your boss came out of it smelling of roses,' I said. 'Trying the kiss of life on his old enemy! Without success, of course.'

If Jim had any doubts about the sincerity of the Colonel's efforts at resuscitation, he was too much of the old school to be disloyal to a good employer. 'It's a pity there was only himself and the ambulancemen there to bear him out. When I got there, I was surprised not to see the Parkers. They'd passed me not long before on the path that runs along the ridge.'

'Which Parkers would that be?' I asked him.

'The couple that have the small house set back from the main road by the bridge at Sprauchlefuird. Ford House, it's called.'

His words brought to my mind a memory of a picturesque house with a floriferous garden rather run to

81

seed, set against towering trees within a curl of stream. 'I know the place. An attractive spot.'

'Which is more than you can say for either of them,' Jim said. 'What they live on, the good Lord only knows. Maybe they've private means or else he took early retirement. Most of their time's spent walking a fat spaniel over McInsch House land, trying to let the fumes of the drink blow away, I've no doubt. The smell of it on their breath fairly curls the heather. I've asked them to stick to the paths and so has the Colonel, but they won't. With no laws of trespass in Scotland . . .'

I nodded sympathetically. 'You'd have to get an interdict against each of them,' I said.

'Not a hope of that. We'd have to prove that the dog was uncontrollable. But it's not. It's just that they don't fash thesselves to control it. Here's me going round the boundaries ilka morning, dogging-in the birds, and they come round after and bloody well dog them out again. Some damn fine rows we've had about it, I can tell you.'

Many keepers would have found ways to deal with such a dog. Indeed, I could think of one animal which had been found among sheep with a bullet in its ribs and a strand of wool in its teeth. But Jim, with his regard for the law, would never have stooped to such means.

Jim had had his digression but he was not going to get away with it. 'You may have the Colonel around a lot more after the next election,' I said. 'I don't see him even being nominated again if he goes on getting himself talked about. I've heard more than one person say that he could have kept Ken Berry alive if he'd tried harder. And there are whispers that the alibi he swore to, when you were accused of poisoning raptors, was a little bit less than kosher.'

Jim's face was a picture. It showed consternation

mingled with guilt and just a touch of satisfaction. 'There was absolutely no truth in the charges against me,' he snapped, 'and that's all I have to say on the matter.'

'I never thought that there was any truth in them,' I said, 'and nor does anybody else. That isn't in question. You've never had any more visits from your accusers?'

'That's one pair we did get interdicted and the court extended the interdict to cover the whole of the Colonel's land,' Jim said. I waited. He had evaded the question and he knew it and in the end he sighed. 'There's a public footpath crosses the land,' he said. 'I've seen yon Dennis Pratt on it with a stalker's telescope. But if he thinks he'll spot me poisoning sparrow-hawks he's barking up the wrong tree.'

Even after his narrow escape from conviction, Jim's faith in the law was such that he still thought that innocence was a sufficient defence. 'All the same,' I said, 'you'd better go canny. They trumped up a charge against you. The tables were turned on them.'

'They asked for a' that they got and more.'

'Maybe. You feel that the end justified the means. But maybe they were convinced that you really were poisoning sparrowhawks and that they were justified in faking the evidence to prove the truth. In which case, they might think that the end would justify the means and it would be only justice if you were to be convicted, second time out, and they would be vindicated. If I were you, I'd try to have an independent witness with me whenever I visited my traps.'

He nodded sadly. 'That's good thinking. I don't like it a damn bit, but it's sound.'

'Did you ever wonder whether Ken Berry mightn't be behind them?' I asked.

Jim shrugged. 'Aye. Often, but there's no way of telling. He was friendly enough wi' me at the time. It could've been his sly way of making trouble for the Colonel.'

'I'm told that Mr Berry was pally with one of them. It seems a queer sort of friendship for a shooting man.'

'Mr Berry used to contribute, whenever they came round collecting for animal charities. Not if they were wanting money to support crackpots and saboteurs, he drew the line at that. It was just his way of keeping them off his back. That way, when the antis went on the warpath it'd be agin somebody else. He subscribed as much or more to the hunt.' Jim glanced at the clock on the wall. 'And now, the pub's open. I've time for one afore I have to be getting back.'

'Or maybe two?' I said, getting out the keys.

He grinned. 'Maybe. But no more than that. It's all right for some, living over the shop, but I've to drive.'

Behind the glass of the door I hung the notice which Deborah had patiently lettered for us some years earlier. We crossed the Square and established ourselves with a drink apiece in a corner of the hotel's public bar, empty at that hour. 'Is your fishing let just now?' I asked.

'No' that I ken of,' he said. 'I've seen nobody at the water for days. And I'd have known. The water's not really my business but I'm often called on to act as ghillie if a client wants it and even if I'm not needed himself tries to mind to give me warning, because I keep an eye out for poachers and he'd not want me challenging a fishing tenant. Why do you ask?'

'Curiosity,' I said. 'I did the Colonel a favour a few days ago. His solicitor suggested that instead of a cash reward I might be given a day or two on the McInsch House water, but your boss has been backward about coming forward. I was wondering why.'

'Damned if I know,' Jim said. 'If the fishing's not let, it'd be no skin off his nose if you tried your hand. He's never gone near the water himself since Mr Berry died except to walk the dogs along the bank. There's precious few salmon coming through just now anyway.' He grinned suddenly. 'But I'll tell you something. I have a written agreement with the Colonel and we've aye stuck to the letter of it. Under the clause about me having the right to a keeper's day for the beaters at the end of the shooting season, I've the right to fish the water and to give a certain number of invites to the fishing on days when it's not let. That's a clause left over from the days of my predecessor and no' one I've taken advantage of until now, because I get plenty of chances to fish while I'm ghillying. They like to go home, you see, and say, "We got this many fish between us," not mentioning that the ghillie helped fill the bag. But there's no reason I shouldn't. If you've a fancy to fish the water, give me a ring beforehand. But I'll warn you, there's hardly a salmon to be seen, looking down from the hill.'

'I'd only be after trout,' I said. 'I wouldn't want to use a two-handed rod just yet.'

'Likely enough,' Jim said. He studied his empty glass. 'My shout. You'll take the other half?'

I said that I could manage another glass of the house red and Jim fetched replacements.

'I hear you had a bust-up at McInsch House,' I said tentatively.

Jim looked puzzled for a moment and then sighed. 'You mean young Nick? Aye. The Colonel's down in the mouth – Nick was his last reminder of his lady. But there was an argy-bargy, I don't know over what, and out goes Nick on his ear. I'm sad for the Colonel. I thought he was maybe changing his mind, but not a bit of it. Maybe it's as well in the long run, even if it has left the Colonel to rattle around on his own in the big, empty house. I never did trust that Nick. Even as a loon, he was aye sleekit.'

As far as I knew I had never encountered Nick

Lamontine, but from something Keith had said I had gathered that he was indeed a slippery character. 'We had a lady in the shop looking for a birthday present for Nick,' I said. 'A blonde.'

'With green eyes and a pointy face?' Jim looked disapproving and at the same time amused. 'There's some would say she *was* his birthday present. That would be Mrs Ritson-Jones. Her father's a landowner down by Kelso,' he said. Like any Scot older than television, he took conversation as a fine art and would fluff out any subject by exploring the identity and relationships of every character cropping up in it. The next few minutes was taken up with brief biographies of Mrs Ritson-Jones's nearer relatives. 'She's divorced now and back living with her dad,' Jim resumed at last. 'She's been hanging around Nick for months and it can't be for what she can get out of him. She has expensive tastes, that lady.'

'She bought him a nice priest. Was he pleased with it?'

Jim, caught in the act of raising his glass, managed half a shrug. 'His birthday was afore the big tiff, but he never said. And unless the Colonel relents I don't see Nick affording the salmon fishing – I've heard him girning to his uncle that his earnings would barely keep him alive. And at his best he's little chance of catching a fish to tap on the head with yon priest. He ties a nice fly but he couldn't cast one into the branches of a tree if you put him under it, for all the hours I've spent trying to teach him to cast. He'd be as well saving his money and doing his fishing in the swimming pool behind the Recreation Centre. No, the most use he'll have for the priest will be for his sea-fishing, where he only has to drop his line over the side of a boat, or to fight off the local sluts. He was aye a man for the ladies and there's a few of those are aye on the lookout for a manly young fellow with no wife of his own.'

'Perhaps a rich divorcee is just what he needs,' I suggested.

Jim drained his glass but before getting up he paused to consider my suggestion. He shook his head firmly. 'A divorcee she may be, but rich, never. The signs are all there. Good clothes, but none of them fresh – either she's had them a while or they're from the Nearly New shop. A small car of her own, away past its best, and if she turns up in a shiny new Volvo estate it'll be her dad's, that's not a woman's car. And I wouldn't know, but Mrs Watson, the housekeeper, says that her jewellery's paste. It would've fooled me, but Mrs Watson was dresser to the Duchess of Caithness and she knows jewels the way I know shotguns. I'm in no doubt the lady's dependent on her dad; and it's changed days for landowners, the money to be earned out of the land isn't what it used to be. A fine new car to show the neighbours but mince and tatties in the dining-room.'

'The money's in different hands these days,' I agreed. During my years as Keith's partner I had seen the shop's clientele change. We saw the same faces, but the expensive rods and guns were bought now by the faces that had once made do with mass-produced second-best.

Jim sighed. 'It's high time I wasn't here,' he said, getting to his feet. 'Mind now, when you want a day's fishing, phone me. There's a few wild brownies, and some of the rainbows the laird put in a couple of years back may still be around.'

'I shan't forget,' I told him. 'And thanks.'

SIX

On the following day, Keith was engaged at his work-bench at home but Molly took over the shop and we were free for our planned outing of investigation.

If Janet had previously been half-hearted about the hunt for the blonde woman, her attitude changed when I mentioned Jim's revelation of the other woman's name as being Mrs Ritson-Jones. As soon as the flat was in a moderately passable state for the day she gathered up the makings of a picnic snack, dressed herself for the country in a jersey, stout shoes and a loose skirt of light tweed and many pleats, checked that I had my medication in my pocket and then fairly hounded me down to the car. Usually the slowest of drivers, she left Newton Lauder as if from a starting grid.

'When did Mrs Ritson-Jones rattle your cage?' I asked her.

'I don't know what you mean.'

'Yes, you do. You're not acting out of curiosity, for once, nor hoping to help out Mr Enterkin or Colonel McInsch. From the moment I mentioned Mrs Ritson-Jones, you've seemed like a disaster looking for the right person to happen to. And,' I added as she over-took another car in the teeth of oncoming traffic, 'slow down unless you can't wait to see my next coronary.'

Janet slowed a little. 'I have never met the person,' she said.

'That doesn't matter. I have an intense dislike of several persons I've never met.'

'Like who?'

I used my Nitrolingual spray. Janet took the hint and slowed down until she was almost within the legal speed limit. 'Various politicians,' I said, 'especially the ones who seem to think that nobody notices when they avoid the question or tell downright lies. People who make trousers that don't come up over the hips or paintbrushes that shed their hairs or anything else that doesn't do its job properly. Several game-show hosts. Anyone who says that he'll do something and then doesn't. I could go on.'

'No wonder you're having blood-pressure problems,' Janet said. 'What you've just said covers about three-quarters of the human race. Well, all right. I've never met her, I've only seen her at a distance, but I hate her guts. I used to know Johnny Ritson-Jones. He belonged near here. We used to knock around together before you came along.'

'You'd hardly left school when I came along,' I pointed out.

'I know. You were a cradle-snatcher,' Janet said complacently. Reliving the past, she had let the car slow down to an almost reasonable speed. 'But with Johnny it was nothing serious, I was only in my teens and he was years older, we just happened to dance well together and laugh at the same sort of things. He wasn't a randy sort of man but he liked to have a girl to flirt with, and I had a driving licence and didn't drink, so he used to take me out dining and clubbing and to drive him home. It was a lot of fun for a young girl and an educational experience, if you know what I mean. And he had some really fun cars for me to drive him home in. I thought that I was madly in love with him.'

'And were you?'

'Maybe I was, in a romantic sort of way. But I was also very innocent until you came along and Johnny was always the perfect gentleman, or else he didn't fancy me that way, so you needn't be jealous.'

'I'm not.'

Janet, who had been looking dreamily through the windscreen, laughed and accelerated again. 'I don't know that I find that exactly flattering. Anyway, it might have gone on until I was old enough to marry and we could have lived happily ever after. But I suppose Johnny had the same needs as the next man and he met Joanna Ritson-Jones – Joanna Hickson she was then – at some party that I wasn't asked to. And that was that,' Janet said grimly, her smile gone. 'She set her cap at him. They sent me an invitation to their wedding. I didn't go, of course, but I saved up all my pocket money for ages and ages and sent them a crystal bowl and on their wedding night I went to bed early and wept into my pillow.'

I felt a pang of pity for the teenager who had cried into her pillow but when I put my hand over hers on the wheel she shook it off brusquely. 'Later, I heard that she led him an awful dance as well as running through his money in the end and then running out on him. There was a divorce. He was killed in a car smash soon after that, probably because he didn't care a lot whether he lived or died. So, yes, you could say that she rattled my cage. Is this where we turn off?'

'Next on the left.' I glanced from the map to her face and saw a tear on her cheek. 'I'm sorry,' I said. 'I thought that Keith was your first love.'

'Keith was different,' she said stiffly. 'He treated me as though I was six years old. He still does sometimes.' She cleared her throat, removed the tear with the back of her hand leaving a smudge behind and made the turn. 'Damn all men. Damn everybody. Where do we go now?'

'Follow your freshly unpowdered nose to the T-junction,' I said.

Janet snorted and leaned over for a quick glance at herself in the rear-view mirror. She halted when we arrived at the T-junction, ostensibly to argue about the route but in fact to get out her powder compact.

If the map was to be trusted, there were six farms on the road that ran left from the T-junction, but no isolated houses nor farmhouse cottages. We turned that way first. Two of the farmhouses were derelict and roofless, but it took us until after midday to investigate the others because it was necessary first to observe from a distance for signs of any of our quarry or of cars resembling those used by them and thereafter to approach with a carefully fabricated version of the bad-debt story. One boy with a bicycle was fairly sure that he had seen the Rover, but when pressed was quite unable to say where or when.

We parked on a broad verge near the T-junction and carried our picnic up a small knoll. Janet insisted on doing the carrying. While she spread a cloth over the car rug I studied the view, which took in a great swath of the best of Borders scenery. High cloud was taking the heat out of the summer sun but the air was sharp and clear all the way to the Cheviots. The stream where Johnson and I had fished a couple of days earlier, marked by a long chain of treetops, led away down the middle of a broad valley to where it joined the river, two miles away across country but a dozen or more by road.

I could make out both McInsch House and Berry Castle in the middle distance. At that range they looked amicable and not in the least as though their occupants had a deeply ingrained habit of quarrelling. Ken Berry's son, we had been given to understand, was shortly to return from New Zealand where he had been in charge of some ramification of a family business. I wondered whether the eternal feud was to be included in his inheritance. It seemed unlikely, if for no other reason than that Ken Berry's death and the Colonel's lack of direct descendants surely broke the chain.

'We could be on a wild-goose chase,' I said as I helped myself to salad. 'She may only have come up here for a few minutes. She may have brought her accomplices here to look down at McInsch House in case there was a signal, a sheet in Nick Lamontine's window or something like that, meaning "The money's in the house" or "Meet me at dusk" or "Listen in for a message" or whatever. It could explain why there hasn't been much suspicious traffic on the CB radio.'

I had to point out McInsch House to Janet and then go back to the car for my binoculars before she would accept that messages could be passed that way. 'But he was already away from there before you saw her coming up here,' she said.

'She might not have known that.'

Janet had stuffed tomatoes with cottage cheese, which proved delicious. I made a good lunch while she watched McInsch House through my binoculars without removing them from her eyes even to eat. 'There is a sheet or something at a window,' she said suddenly.

'But Nick Lamontine isn't there.'

'Maybe there's been a reconciliation that we don't know about.'

'You've got egg on your chin,' I told her sleepily. It was not much of an answer but it saved me from getting into one of those mind-taxing discussions full of ifs and buts. I could have settled down for a nap, but Janet wanted to get on and soon haled me back to the car.

According to the map, there were only two farms on the other side of the T-junction. We drove to the end of the road, where we could overlook a small farmhouse with a large garden which seemed to be swarming with children together with two women in deckchairs. If even half of the visible humans were permanent residents, there would be no room for lodgers.

Near the T-junction a narrow farm-road led away south and a faded sign promised that the last small farm shown on the map was to be found there, hidden by the contours. Although there were signs of the recent passage of vehicles, the farm-road had received no maintenance for years, so that weather and the passage of farm machinery had reduced it to a surface of ruts and boulders over which a car would need to be nursed with care and a hardened heart. Our car was nearly new and had a low ground clearance. Janet parked it at the roadside but out of harm's way.

'According to the map,' she said, 'it's only a quarter of a mile. Can you walk that far?'

'I could walk ten times as far,' I told her. 'Just don't hurry me.'

We stepped over a sagging fence and set off across a field of grass. As we walked, a roof began to rise beyond the first crest and before we had gone a hundred yards we could see that it belonged to a barn-like building, traditionally built with stone gables, timber walls to front and back and a slated roof. This was in doubtful condition. Many slates were missing and the roof had settled enough to show the lines of the main trusses, giving the barn rather the look of a hungry dog. Beyond it, the view over the Borders opened up again.

The building seemed low, as if it had sunk into the ground under its own considerable weight, but as we neared a wide, open doorway we saw through the openings on the other side that the ground beyond was much lower and that we were entering what had once been a hayloft. Further off, the farmhouse was a roofless shell, long abandoned, but when it was inhabited, I thought idly, it must have had a splendid outlook – not that a farmer and lifelong occupant would look at the view except to oversee his crops and cattle.

The loft, it seemed, was still in occasional use as storage by whichever farmer still worked the land, because fencing wire and posts were stacked along the near wall and I nearly fell over the tool used for making holes for fence posts and known locally as a 'podger'.

It seemed unlikely that the place had been of any interest to Mrs Ritson-Jones and her partners, except perhaps as an observation post overlooking McInsch House. I was about to turn back but Janet, more determined or more curious, walked forward, intending to look down from the edge of the large opening through which hay had formerly been forked down to the beasts below.

It seemed to me that the ancient floor, which had never been of anything more substantial than pine and had been subjected to a generation of rain blowing through the wall openings or leaking through the roof above, was in deplorable condition. It was noticeable that any use made of it by the present occupier was kept close to the near wall. I also saw that rotten boards had sometimes been replaced with narrower ones and through the gaps I could see what might have been some sort of van under the large opening, its roof only a foot or two below the beams. Dark stains with pale edges suggested that strands of wood rot were continuing their work on the boards.

I hesitated for a moment between an urgent desire

to call Janet back and a reluctance to announce our presence. And while I still hesitated, it was already too late. Janet trod on a rotten section of the floor. There was a soft rending noise. One foot and then both legs began to disappear. Fragments pattered down below and Janet cried out in shock. She was supporting herself on her elbows over the joists on either side, as an alternative to falling through to the floor beneath. From the jerking of her upper half, her nether regions were kicking violently but to no purpose.

If I had rushed to her aid I might have made matters worse. I began to pick my way carefully, guessing at the positions of the joists and trying to keep my weight over them.

Below us, I heard the door of the van slide back and a man's voice shout with laughter. Janet's eyebrows shot up. 'Joanna!' the voice cried. 'Well, hello my darling! I didn't know it was Christmas.'

As I reached Janet, she began to struggle more furiously. But her pleated skirt had spread around her. It was under her hands and elbows, preventing her from pushing herself up from the floor. She could not have held up her hands to me without falling through. I made sure that I had a sound foothold on bare boards, grabbed her under the armpits and pulled. She stuck for a moment and then came up like a cork out of a bottle.

As I set her on her feet, I found that I was looking down into the face of the black-haired man with the boxer's nose, who stood with one hand still raised, the grin frozen on his face. Behind him, I saw that the van was a neat motor caravan. I gave Janet a push towards the door by which we had come in. She straightened her clothing with angry twitches as she went.

The man spun round and darted into the van. I could only guess at what he was after – a weapon, reinforcements or transport – but I was sure that we would be better off if he remained without it. I took three paces to the wall and lifted the podger. This was a long and heavy bar of round steel, sharpened at one end and at the other swelling into a metal ball for added weight. I lugged it to the brink above the caravan, lifted it with an effort and sent it down like a spear. Whether it killed the man, nailed the van to the ground or otherwise disabled it I neither knew nor cared just so long as there was no immediate pursuit. I did not even wait to see the result. As I fled, I heard a crunch of metal and a furious roar from below.

I grabbed Janet's hand and we ran for the car.

Janet was puzzled, trusting to my judgement and infected by my haste, but as she fumbled the key into the car's door she asked, 'Was it—?'

I looked back over my shoulder but there was no sign of the man as yet. I was desperate for breath and it occurred to me that this was the first time that I had run since my attack. But at least I could collapse into a seat. 'The man,' I gasped. 'Yes. Let's go.'

She started the engine. 'Go where?'

'Wherever he isn't. Somewhere we can phone the cops from. Or, better, Ralph Enterkin. He'll know what to do.'

Now that the immediate pressure was off, I realized that the excitement and violent effort had triggered a bad attack of angina, the worst yet. With my right hand, because my left was already almost useless, I dug out my Nitrolingual spray and put several squirts onto the underside of my tongue. Another went up my nose as the car bounced in a pothole. The pain became worse, doubled me over.

'Shall I drive straight for the hospital?' Janet asked shakily.

I forced my head up off my knees for a moment. 'How's my colour?' I asked.

She must have taken her eyes off the road for a second. I felt the wheels rumble on the verge. 'I've seen you look worse when you had the flu,' she said.

'It's only angina,' I told her, hoping that I knew what I was talking about. Angina may be unpleasant but it is not a full-blown heart attack. During each attack a piece of the heart dies – a thought which I tried to avoid. 'It'll pass,' I said, to convince myself.

'It had better. You've no business running around like that.'

I used the spray again. The pain steadied but speaking became easier. 'Next time, I'll leave you dangling,' I said.

Without looking up, I could almost feel the heat of her blush. 'With some violent criminal feeling me up from below? I ... hope you did the right thing. It wouldn't have been worth the ultimate sacrifice. Greater love hath no man and all that jazz. Thanks anyway,' she said huskily. A few minutes later, the car slowed to a halt. 'I can phone from somewhere around here. You're sure you won't conk out on me if I leave you for a minute or two?'

'I'll recover quicker if the car stays still for a minute or two,' I told her. I thought that the pain was already beginning to wear off.

By the time Janet came back to the car the pain was no more than a dull ache; and when we arrived in Newton Lauder it was an unpleasant memory. If I was not quite back to my usual self I would have been at least capable of climbing the stairs and resting quietly but, as soon as she had had another word with Mr Enterkin, nothing would do for Janet but to take me to the surgery. My doctor hooked me up to his own miniaturized electrocardiograph before pooh-poohing any idea that I had had a second coronary.

Even so Janet, who had earlier begun to believe that I might eventually be capable of resuming a normal life, had now returned to her previous conviction that my life hung by a thread. She was and is always inclined to overreact. I flatly refused to be tucked up in bed with a hot-water bottle but consented to spend what was left of that particular day in my armchair, because that was exactly what I had intended to do anyway.

In the morning, I averted any attempt to keep me abed by the expedient of getting up and dressed while Janet was still snoring – a very soft and musical snoring like that of a contented kitten, but snoring nevertheless. She accepted the *fait accompli* along with a cup of tea, but made up her mind to keep me at home. I settled down quite readily to my fly-tying. It was easier to sit still now I knew that there could still be wider horizons than allowed by my earlier chairbound existence.

In mid-morning Janet took a phone-call which obviously pleased and stirred her, but she refused at first to relay its contents on the grounds that the excitement might aggravate my condition. When I began to force the issue, she knew perfectly well that my tantrum was a piece of histrionics, but she must have decided that even acting out a burst of temper might raise my blood pressure more than listening in a state of relaxation and so she capitulated, but not before settling us both down with drinks and my medication at hand.

'That was Ralph Enterkin, bringing me up to date,' she said. 'I insisted on his promise to keep us posted before I'd say a word. After I spoke to him the first time, he decided to phone Ian but to avoid any mention of our names or of blackmail and only give him directions to that barn and say that he believed that at least one of two men who were very much wanted by the police could be found there. He mentioned a possible woman accomplice without naming names.'

(Ian, as already mentioned, is Keith's son-in-law and the pinnacle of CID representation in Newton Lauder.)

'He might as well have named Mrs Ritson-Jones,' I said.

'Not without explaining where he got the name from. Mr Enterkin must have warned Ian that the man could be violent, because Ian gathered up a posse that needed two cars to transport them. They found the barn. Apparently you had spiked the van to the ground and also mucked up its wiring. The man was trying to get it going again when the police sneaked up on him. He tried to bluff it out, but he was too much like the videofit of one of the men who have been raiding building societies between here and Edinburgh for the last few weeks, so Ian wasn't buying any stories. Then one of the policemen found a sawn-off shotgun hidden in the barn and that was more or less that as far as the first man was concerned.

'They lay in wait. The second man never turned up and they think that he may have taken fright when he failed to get an answer over the CB radio.' Janet paused and produced her happiest smile. 'The only arrival was Joanna Ritson-Jones. She tried to make out that she had only just met the man for the first time a few days ago and knew nothing about his activities, but a woman had been driving for the two raiders and there were traces of a woman's presence in the motor caravan which Ian thinks Forensics will connect with her, although,' Janet said reluctantly, 'she doesn't seem to have been sleeping there. Her story is that she was there because she was negotiating to buy the motor caravan. But they have enough to hold her in custody. Would you believe that she had the nerve to ask Mr Enterkin to be her solicitor? He told her to sod off, or words to that effect. They recovered a whole lot of money that they think will be traceable back to the building societies.

'And one other thing. The man they're holding—'

'The one who was so pleased to see you in the barn,' I said.

Janet flushed. *'The man they're holding* has been very close-mouthed but they tricked him into letting something slip. The information about the movement of the money didn't reach them from a local source. He was only the muscle and he doesn't know the whole story but he's sure that instructions were reaching them from Edinburgh.'

'Well, we've made somebody happy,' I said, 'even if he doesn't know that it was us.'

Janet beamed at me. 'If you mean Ian, we can spring it on him some day when we want a favour.'

'Maybe.' I held my peace and my breath while I set a pair of wings into a Mayfly. 'So that's an end to it,' I said.

'I expect so,' said Janet. She got up and went through into the kitchen.

After the excitement of that day and the penalty paid in chest pains, I was content to live quietly for a week or two, manning the shop when required but otherwise relaxing, tying flies for my own collection or for friends and drifting over to the hotel for a drink with the same friends whenever the idea occurred to anybody. The CB radio seemed to have run out of mysterious and cryptic messages, but it was still in use so that I could be monitored from time to time whenever I was alone. If sometimes this made me feel like an irritable goldfish I was also soothed by the knowledge that my friends cared enough to bother. One unambitious venture with Johnson Laing after trout produced several reasonable fish and a comfortable reassurance that escape was still available whenever I was strong-minded and rash enough to grasp for it. On the whole, the fact that escape was possible was escape enough.

One Thursday, Keith was due in Edinburgh again

and Janet, who had been going around with an abstracted air, decided that she had errands to do. I took over the shop in mid-morning, occasionally reassuring Molly over the CB radio all the way to Briesland House, and, it being our day for early closing, locked up at lunchtime and walked over to the hotel for a bar meal.

Ralph Enterkin, when already past middle age, had amazed one and all by marrying a widowed barmaid. To the greater amazement of the community, this had proved to be one of its most successful marriages. Mrs Enterkin, a plump and jolly yet very feminine woman, was behind the bar. Knowing of old that any assumption on the part of bar staff that I would have again today whatever I had had every day for years past provoked an immediate desire to wait until it was served and then order something different, she waited for my nod before putting out a glass of the house red and passing an order to the kitchen.

A minor reason for the success of the Enterkin partnership was that Mrs Enterkin had a talent for absorbing all the local gossip and passing it on to nobody but her husband, to his great professional advantage. She would probably know more than anybody about such things as the drowning of Ken Berry, but she could be very discreet, especially about matters in which her husband was concerned, so I took my wine to a corner table and waited without any great enthusiasm for the arrival of my meal. The worst snag to the aftermath of my coronary, I had found, was that a low-fat, low-cholesterol diet precluded almost any food with an enjoyable taste. Only the fact that occasional indulgence in such delicacies as bacon and eggs was now spiced with a delicious taint of guilt which I imagined was ordinarily reserved for extramarital affairs made deprivation endurable.

My cold ham and salad had arrived and I was trying

not to think about steaks or pork chops when a fresh arrival chased all thoughts of gastronomy out of my mind. A woman's voice said, 'Do you mind if I join you?' and I looked up to see a blonde woman taking possession of the chair opposite me.

Her face was sharp, even hawkish when seen close to, and by the slight slackness of her skin I guessed that she was older than I thought. My previous glimpses of Mrs Ritson-Jones had been distant and fleeting and it took me a few seconds to be sure that this was the same person. She looked less immaculate, although I could not have pinpointed any differences except that her parting was showing a streak of dull brown.

It was too late for getting up even if I had felt like rising for a woman whom I knew to be less than trustworthy, although I had cause to be grateful that her predation had resulted in Janet still being available when I came on the scene. I emptied my mouth. She was already seated so that there was nothing left for me to do or say but smile graciously.

Studying her for the first time, I could see the underlying signs that Jim Waterhouse had mentioned. Her dress, which showed signs of wear and looked slightly dated to my inexpert eye, had once been good and had been chosen to show off an attractive figure to best advantage. Her makeup was cleverly shaded, turning a face which when I looked behind the façade was both hard and sharp into an illusion of softness and beauty. All in all, she showed every sign of being not only a dangerous woman but one who was skilled in the wiles of womanhood. The clear drink in front of her might have been water but I thought not.

At the moment, however, she seemed less than sure of herself. After a moment's hesitation she said, 'You're Janet's husband, aren't you?'

It was not the title to which I generally liked to answer, but I said that I was.

'I'd like to ask you something.' She looked into my eyes. Her eyes were her best feature, deep and limpid, and she knew how to use them to register frankness and sincerity. 'Is there any reason why you shouldn't tell me why you were watching us, that day outside the bank?'

I have an instinctive distrust of anyone who can register frankness and sincerity so convincingly, but offhand I could think of at least one reason why I wanted to satisfy her desire for enlightenment. If she and one of her playmates were running around loose, I would prefer them not to believe that we had been part of a wholesale plot against them. 'You go first,' I said. I rather hoped that the pause that followed, which was part of my mental drill for beating my usual stammer, would be taken for the reserve of the strong, silent man. 'Tell me how you come to be here instead of enjoying the hospitality of our police.'

After one hurt glance, 'I'm on bail,' she snapped. But I guessed that she had taken the point. If I had to ask, I could not be hand in glove with the police.

'And your friends?'

'Please don't call them that. They're no friends of mine and they never were. They caught me when I was broke and offered me money in exchange for some news from my boyfriend about his father. They said it was for a journalist. There didn't seem to be any harm in it. Then I found that I had been sucked into something really crooked and there was no way out, not without risking arrest on the one hand and being thumped on the other.'

'That doesn't answer my question,' I said.

Her eyes sparked for a moment but she contained her temper. 'Doug's still inside. The . . . other hasn't shown up. It doesn't look as if either of them would have a hope in hell of getting bail. Each of them jumped bail in the past at least once. Does that earn me an answer?'

'It was purest chance,' I told her. 'I'd been listening in to the CB radio for quite another reason and picked up your messages. Our local knowledge suggested that Ralph Enterkin was a target. He's our friend. We weren't going to let him get mugged.'

She nodded slowly. 'When I saw Janet staring at me I knew her straight away although I hadn't set eyes on her for about ten years.' (By my reckoning it had to be more like twenty, but I allowed her her petty vanity.) 'We'd never met, but my late husband' – she managed to look as though for two pins she could have shed a tear – 'pointed her out to me once. Seeing her again like that, and she isn't the sort you can forget, I thought that we'd been set up, or why else would somebody who could identify me be gawping at the front of the hotel? Then I realized that she was nothing to do with the fuzz and I thought it had to be just lousy luck.'

'We thought that you must have given up the whole idea,' I said.

'It was decided – not by me, I was a pawn, if that – decided that lifting the money here was too dangerous. They were going to go after it on its way to the hand-over. How did you come to be at the barn?'

'I'd gone fishing near there and I saw you drive past.'

'As simple as that!' She saw that my glass was empty and picked it up. 'Don't move,' she said.

'I've had enough red wine for the moment,' I said.

'I'm sure you could manage a brandy.'

She got up and moved to the bar with a swaying walk that I was sure had been cultivated with care. It certainly gathered up every male eye in the place.

I sat where I was and finished my meal. No doubt

she would want something, but if a woman with some pretension to beauty – though perhaps not as much as she thought she had – wanted to ply me with drink, and under the eyes of a number of admiring locals, why not? I could always refuse whatever favour she was after. Meantime, why should Keith always be the partner to whom a reputation for dalliance seemed to arrive of its own accord? Janet, I told myself firmly, would understand.

The brandy that she brought back with her was at least a double although I noticed that she was still nursing her own original drink. She sat down and gathered up my attention with the skill of a sailor coiling rope. 'I need a favour,' she said. (I made no comment. That fact had been obvious from the outset.) 'I want somebody to speak to that damned lawyer for me.'

'Ralph Enterkin?'

'That one. He won't see me and he won't take my phone-calls and I'm not going to commit myself to writing.'

'Seeing that you were – allegedly, as they say – part of a team that was going to hijack a scad of clients' money off him, presumably with violence, can you blame him?'

She shrugged. Evidently that little matter was in the past, and if she could put it behind her Mr Enterkin would be showing up in a poor light if he failed to do the same. 'I can do a deal if he'll only listen to me. I've lived most of my life in these parts and I know about him. He's good. Not only that, but by reputation he's straight. He's not one of those lawyers who'll grab the money and try to get some habitual child-molester off the hook by arguing some obscure point of law. When he defends somebody, he means it; and he's well known for it, so he gets believed. They don't have a strong case against me. If he handles it, he could get me off –

especially if I drop those other two sods deep in it. But I'm not going to do that unless I'm damn sure they're going to go down.'

'By which,' I said, 'you mean that those others already suspect that you may have landed them in the soup?'

'They were blaming me for the fiasco outside here,' she said frankly. 'And they're rough. If you even play Tiddlywinks with them you're risking a broken arm. I haven't seen either of them since Doug was grabbed at the barn, but I can guess what they're thinking.'

'So can I. If Ralph Enterkin decides to represent you, what can you offer in return?'

'You won't go running to the police?' When I shook my head, she went on. 'I can give him enough information to sink those two for keeps, the identity of the other man and a good enough idea of where to look for him.'

'That's information that you'll have to divulge anyway if you want them kept off your neck.'

A shadow passed over her face and was gone again. 'I can give him the identity of the witnesses against his client, the immaculate Colonel Ivor McInsch MP.'

Although my conscious mind had been determined to forget about blackmail and general wickedness, it seemed that my subconscious had been chewing on the known facts and had come to a more or less logical conclusion. 'Mr and Mrs Parker at Sprauchlefuird?' I said.

As I said the words I decided that they were a reasonable guess. Although Ken Berry's death might not be at the heart of the blackmail attempt, the Parkers had cause to dislike the Colonel and spent much of their time walking his land. Even if they had not witnessed the drowning they might well have made a damning statement about that or something else, either tricked by the journalist or out of spite.

Mrs Ritson-Jones's face twitched once but was then fully under control. I knew then that I had guessed well. That information itself was less significant than the fact that she knew it.

'You can't expect me to comment,' she said quickly.

'No,' I said. 'I don't.' I decided to leave her with the impression that Mr Enterkin already knew the identity of the accusers, which for all I knew might have been the case. 'Now, if you could fill in the details of just what sort of accusation they're making and how far they can back it up, I might be able to persuade him. No guarantees, mind, but I could try.'

'Well, no guarantees, but I could try to find out,' she said. 'I have a possible source.'

'You're still in touch with Nick Lamontine, then?' I said. 'I thought there had been a bust-up.'

Once again a brief flicker of pain showed on her face. I was only having a little quiet fun while indulging in a series of educated guesses, at the same time exacting just a little revenge on behalf of Janet and her lost love; but it must have seemed to her that all her best cards were already out on the table.

'The bust-up was between Nick and his stepfather,' she said. 'And I can tell you something about that. It was Nick who set your pal Enterkin up. Not directly. Sid Jubilee—'

'The journalist?' I asked quickly. I had seen the name on a byline somewhere.

'That's right. It was Jubilee who put pressure on Nick to listen in on calls. Nick didn't want to do it. Somebody should tell the Colonel that. I don't know what the leverage was, but it must have been something heavy. I might be able to find out from Nick. He'd sell his soul for a touch of the old such-and-such.' She named a sexual practice of which I had only heard without even managing to visualize it. I hoped to God that we were not being overheard by any of the other drinkers present.

'I believe you,' I said sincerely. My ears felt hot.

She recovered an air of superior amusement which I later learned was normal to her. 'Now I've shocked you,' she said. 'If Janet's too prim to do you that little favour, she can't have enjoyed being ogled by Doug Waller. They tell me that he's come round to seeing the funny side of it now. He thought at the time that it was me dangling through the floor above him.'

'Until she tried to kick him away,' I said.

It took her a second or two to find the insult hidden in my words. Her mouth hardened. 'Whatever you think of me, the other offer stands. I'll see what I can find out. You sound out your solicitor pal and we'll see if we can't do a trade.'

'How do I get in touch with you?' I asked. 'Are you staying here?'

She gave a mirthless laugh. 'At these prices? You don't get in touch with me. I'll give you a call.' She smiled naturally for the first time, showing a trace of what must once have ensnared Johnny Ritson-Jones. 'If Janet answers, I'll hang up,' she said.

She got to her feet and left the lounge bar, again deliberately drawing all the male eyes to the sway of her hips. I nursed the remains of my brandy for a minute or two and then followed.

SEVEN

Out in the fresh air and daylight, I almost bumped into Mr Enterkin. Catching my eye, he slowed and halted.

'I think that we should have a word together,' I said.

'Over a dram, perhaps?' he suggested, glancing at the double doors from which I had just emerged.

The idea was tempting, but if I took any more alcohol I would probably do something stupid. And I had never had enough strength of mind to sit in a bar and drink tonic water. 'I have to get home,' I said, 'or Janet will worry. Phone me?'

'I must have two words with my good lady. I could follow you to your home after that.'

'Fine.'

I crossed the Square and took my time climbing the stairs. Janet had returned and seemed to be noisily rearranging everything in the kitchenette, a sure sign that all was not well.

I sat down at my fly-dressing table, determined to keep my head down until the clouds had passed. My table was tidier now. Keith had brought me a cabinet of small drawers from his workshop (slightly stained with oil from the tools and small components for which it had been made), into which had gone my steadily increasing collection of hooks, feathers, silks, hairs and synthetics.

After a few minutes, Janet came through and headed

for the wall cupboard where we kept our drinks. She looked a question.

'Don't tempt me,' I said. 'I've been in the hotel.'

'Ah.' She poured herself a large gin-and-nothing, put it down carefully on the coffee table and dropped into one of the fireside chairs with her back to me. 'I think I've just made an ass of myself,' she said loudly.

Out of my years of experience I could tell that whatever I said would be wrong, so I held my peace. After a long pause she went on more gently. 'Only having bits of the story has been driving me mad, like putting down a mystery novel in the middle or hearing the first half of a piece of music. After we pulled out all the stops to be helpful, we were left in the dark about who was blackmailing the Colonel, about what and whether he really did whatever it was. And I remembered what you'd said Jim Waterhouse told you and I made a guess that the missing witnesses were—' She broke off at the sound of footfalls on the stair.

'Mr and Mrs Parker,' I said. I would have called the words back if I could. While Janet was in a mood to kick herself, it would have been kinder to allow her to surprise me.

The solicitor chose that moment to rap the knocker on our door. Janet cast up her eyes but she went to let him in. 'It'll be Ralph Enterkin,' I said. Janet told me, through gritted teeth, to stop showing off.

'Don't get up,' said the solicitor, taking the chair opposite me. I thought that friends who would cheerfully have sought my help to change a wheel were always determined to keep me sitting down. Janet brought another dining chair to my table and fetched her gin. 'While I'm on my feet,' she said, 'can I fetch anyone a drink?'

'No more for me,' I said.

'Then I shall keep you company in your abstinence,'

Enterkin said. 'You wanted a word with me?'

I said that I did.

'Let me go first,' Janet said. 'I was going to phone you anyway, because I may have rushed in where angels fear to tread. I meant well. I thought I was being clever. But I . . . I wasn't.' The last two words were choked out.

Mr Enterkin sighed. 'Tell me,' he said.

Janet took a pull at her drink. 'After we found that man in the barn,' she said, turning faintly pink, 'Wal was in pain and I couldn't be sure that it was angina and not another full-blown heart attack, so I stopped at the first house on the main road and called the surgery, mostly to be sure there was a doctor there. I spoke to the doctor and he said that it sounded like angina but to bring him in anyway. I was too steamed up to think logically at the time, but later I worked it out that it must have been the house where the Parkers live.'

The solicitor was looking puzzled but intrigued. 'Who?' he said. 'What about the Parkers?'

'You and the Colonel have been keen enough to ask for our help,' Janet said with spirit, 'but you've tried not to tell us anything about what was behind it all. But we worked out that it had to be a matter of blackmail and it seemed to me that it had to be something to do with Mr Berry's death.'

'And just how did you work that out?' Ralph Enterkin enquired coldly.

'We have our methods,' Janet said loftily, managing to imply that our logic would be beyond the solicitor's comprehension. 'Obviously we've no way of knowing that the Colonel isn't an undercover member of the Communist Party or has a secret boyfriend or something. It might even hark back to Jim Waterhouse's prosecution. But it seemed far more likely that the fatal accident was at the bottom of it. Whether the Colonel was accused of having delayed pulling him out and starting resuscitation until he was sure that it was too late or whether he was said to have pushed him in in the first place, I wouldn't know.

'Jim Waterhouse, the Colonel's keeper, told Wal that he met the Parkers shortly before all the hoo-ha. They were going down the public footpath towards the river. They must have seen something, yet if they ever came forward as witnesses they weren't called. They've had words with the Colonel in the past, so it seemed to me that if they had seen something, or thought they'd seen something or even thought they could get some money by inventing a story, they could be the secret witnesses.'

'That would seem to be a possibility,' Mr Enterkin agreed. 'Why didn't you tell me?'

'Because you'd said that you'd rather not know. And also because that would have been the end of it. You wouldn't even have told me whether I had guessed right or wrong. So I thought I'd check it out for myself.'

She got up out of her chair and went to refill her glass.

'The road to hell is indeed paved with good intentions,' the solicitor said with a sigh, 'where they should quite properly be trodden underfoot. And did these Parkers indeed prove to be witnesses? My client has been very insistent that I make no enquiries of him or of the – um – journalist concerned as to the nature of the allegations nor the identity of the supposed witnesses. If not content to have my client take over the reins at least I had good reason to bow to his instructions. Compensating a member of the media for the loss of a story may be balanced precariously on the very edge of unprofessional conduct, but paying off a blackmailer is definitely beyond the line – and a very hazy line it can be at times.

'On the other hand, no information is ever to be

sniffed at and my client could hardly instruct me to remain unaware of facts which fall, so to speak, into my lap.

'You may tell me whether these Parkers are in fact the witnesses,' he continued. 'That much may be of use to me. And I think it is now high time that I learned just what the allegations are. My client disagrees, but I would not wish to be able to advise him whether he is right or wrong only in the light of hindsight.'

By this time Janet had seated herself again, but I noticed that she left her refilled glass alone for the moment. Mr Enterkin's convoluted thinking and measured periods seemed to be mind-numbing enough. 'I couldn't tell you, even if I could get a word in edgeways,' she said.

She got up again and prowled restlessly through to the kitchenette to check on her meal. When she came back she was silent until the solicitor said, 'May I suggest that if you intend to say any more, now would be a good time?'

Janet pulled herself together. 'When Wal was taken so bad,' she said, 'I stopped at a house to beg the use of the phone and that gave me a sort of introduction.'

'That would be Chez Parker?' the solicitor suggested.

'So I realized later. I'd noticed a rather fruity smell and there were glasses on the table and bottles on the sideboard, and something Jim Waterhouse said to Wal confirmed that it wasn't a special occasion but that they were regular drinkers.

'So I paid another call, taking along a bottle of brandy as a gift to thank them, as I said, for being so kind and helpful. Actually, they hadn't been kind or helpful, in fact they made me pay for the call while for all they knew my husband was at death's door in the car outside; but they weren't going to turn down the gift of a bottle of good brandy.'

I sat up suddenly and said, 'I wondered where that

113

bottle had gone.' It had been a present from Keith, who has the knack of obtaining luxury goods, always at knock-down or duty-free prices.

'And now you know. You may also care to know that I grudged it almost as much as you seem to do. They're not an attractive couple. He's small and toothy with a lumpy nose and pig's eyes, while she's flabby and over-perfumed. The house smells of the sort of people you wouldn't want to know.

'Well, I hung on like a limpet until they could hardly not offer me a drink out of my own bottle. They left me alone in their sitting-room while they conferred in the hall, obviously discussing how to get rid of me, but all that that achieved was to give me a chance to look at the phone-numbers on the pad by the phone. And I'll tell you something. There were precious few names on it – they don't seem to have any friends – but Ken Berry was there.'

'What about Sid Jubilee?' I asked her.

Mr Enterkin jumped. 'Where did you come across that name?' he demanded.

'Let Janet finish her story,' I suggested.

'Yes, his was one of the names,' Janet said. 'I would have had a job not to get stoned myself, except they seemed to grudge me my share and they were sloshing it down like camels in an oasis. They had the real drinker's knack of not showing it at first, but when I judged that any normal human being would have had to be a long way beyond feeling any pain I tried drop-ping in a casual remark about how sad their neighbour Ken Berry's death had been.

'Neither of them made any direct comment except to agree, with about as much sincerity as a politician forcing himself to kiss a baby, and they got rid of me after that far more quickly than was anything like polite. It isn't easy to put their reaction into words, going only by their expressions, tones of voices and body language, but I'll try. To start with, they weren't a damn bit sorry about Mr Berry but they weren't pleased either; it was the normal reaction of people who don't give a gnat's turd for anybody except themselves. Pardon my French,' Janet added. Her refilled glass was not quite as full as it had been.

'That was on the subject of the actual death. But from that moment on, although they were trying to bustle me out of the place, they seemed a touch more cheerful and now and again a touch of "I know something you don't know" peeped through.'

'*In vino veritas*. You're sure that you're not imagining these subtleties in the light of hindsight?' the solicitor asked her.

'No, of course I'm not sure,' Janet said. 'How could I be? They were hardly acting normally and I'd had one or two myself. But I'm sure that there was something. They knew what I was after. But all they would utter were sort of riddles. "We saw what we saw. Oh yes, we saw them all right!" That sort of thing. But they wouldn't let on what they did see.'

Janet sighed and made a gesture of helplessness. 'As soon as I got back into the car,' she said, 'I tried saying the same things in the same tone of voice and with the same expression on my face. A couple walking a baby and a big dog thought I was mad. And what I just told you was the best interpretation I could arrive at.'

'There have been occasions,' Ralph Enterkin said, 'when I have resorted to similar expedients. Sometimes they work and sometimes they don't.'

The meal was probably forgotten. I went through to the kitchenette and turned down the gas under the potatoes, which were bubbling furiously although still as hard as stones. Everything else seemed to be on course. I went back and sat down. The solicitor was giving Janet a lecture about the dangers of forcing unwanted help on people.

'Don't bully my wife,' I told him. 'Save it for me. I haven't told you why you were invited here in the first place.'

The reminder that he was a guest in our home checked him in mid-diatribe. 'Go on, then,' he said.

'When I met you,' I said, 'I had just parted from Mrs Ritson-Jones. You won't speak to her, so she approached me while I was having a bar lunch, wanting me to act as a go-between. She wants to do a deal. She can sink those other two without trace. Indeed, that's the kingpin of the deal. They think that she shopped them, so she wants them put away – a long way away.'

'And what does she want in return?' Enterkin enquired suspiciously.

'For some strange reason,' I said, 'she seems to think that her chances of getting off would be improved if you were to act for her.'

'Impossible!' he said. He saw me begin to smile and then try to hide it. 'I mean,' he said hotly, 'that it would be impossible for me to represent her.'

'If you say so. But I don't see why.'

'Her interests are adverse to those of my other client, Colonel McInsch.'

'Not any longer.'

Enterkin shifted ground. 'Her two buddies were going to mug me.'

'She isn't charged with that,' I pointed out. 'All that they've got on her is that somebody resembling her was sitting in a car nearby while the two men robbed post offices. If she's prepared to put the police on the track of the missing man and give evidence against the pair of them, you could parlay the charges against her down to where she could get probation. Surely she's entitled to have her side of the case presented as ably as possible?'

'And I get paid out of her share of the proceeds from the post office robberies?'

'Not necessarily. I wouldn't put her chances of collecting her share of the loot above one in fifty. On the other hand, if they turn her down for legal aid she still has a well-heeled daddy. And,' I added, 'she's prepared to find out exactly what the Parkers are alleging against your other client. Surely you have a duty not to turn your back on information which might help him.'

'Oh dear, oh dear, oh dear!' Mr Enterkin said, and he sounded as though he meant it. 'Life can get very complicated. I shall have to go away and think about this.' He heaved himself to his feet. 'And in the meantime, if you should happen to bump into the Colonel, it would be best if you were to say nothing about this. Nothing at all. You understand?'

'I'll talk to him about fishing,' I said agreeably.

'If you must, but not if I am among those present. Also, avoid asking him about access to his bit of the river. He is proving remarkably coy about that. Good day to you.'

I was left to detach Janet from the gin bottle and try to get some solid food into her.

Two days later I had the shop to myself again while Keith was coaching at the local clay-pigeon club.

The day being a Saturday there was a steady trickle of customers but most were in a hurry to get away to their shooting or fishing engagements and by late morning, when the young man came in, the rush was over and the shop was quiet. He was less than prepossessing at first glance, being dark and bullet-headed and running a little to fat, but he was quietly and politely spoken.

We talked absently about the weather and its effect on the fishing while I filled his order. He bought a packet of artificial jungle cock feathers, hooks for tying flies for both salmon and trout and a Kilmore boom that could only have been used for sea fishing. Such a broad span of activity was unusual enough to catch my interest. I knew most of the keen fishermen for miles around, and I only knew of one other whom I had never met.

I put on my most unctuous shopkeeper's manner. 'Did you like the priest the lady bought for you?' I asked him.

He looked at me in surprise and for a moment I had a glimpse of the 'sleekit loon' Jim Waterhouse had described. Then he seemed to give a mental shrug. 'It came from here, did it? It was a pretty thing, but I gave it back to the lady. Not between the eyes, although that was a temptation. I'll get by with my old weighted stag-horn.'

That sounded as though Mrs Ritson-Jones was unlikely to find out much from that source, although when she had last phoned me I had relayed to her a message from Ralph Enterkin provisionally accepting her as a client; but I thought that I might as well check. 'You could tell the lady that we'll take it back from her, if she has no use for it.'

He was still waiting for his change, which I had not yet taken out of the till. There was an unpleasant curl to his rather full upper lip and his manner had shed its polite veneer. 'You don't have to act the innocent,' he said. 'I know that you've been interfering in my stepfather's affairs and I suspect that you put the boot in between me and him. If I find that I'm right I'll come again, and you may get more than a tuppenny-ha'penny priest back. And you needn't think that that bitch will get any more news out of me, because I've chucked her. Now give me my change.'

I gave him his change and he barged out of the shop, knocking over a stand of coarse-fishing equipment as he went. It took me half an hour to restore order and rather longer before I had stopped fuming. Then I remembered that it had indeed been our interference that had convinced the Colonel of his guilt and that, according to Mrs Ritson-Jones, he had been acting under duress. Perhaps he was entitled to dislike me.

Remembering all the advice which had been thrust on me about staying cool and avoiding stress, I forgave his boorishness but with a mental reservation that if it occurred again I would get Janet to beat him up.

On the following Tuesday I was alone in the shop again. Deborah was competing in a major skeet tournament and Keith and Molly had gone off to watch their daughter and to look after their grandchild. Although Janet had insisted on bearing the brunt of the work for a couple of days I had gladly taken over while she made an assault on our laundry.

It was a quiet morning, redeemed by the visits of an old client wanting to discuss the relative merits of various salmon reels and of a man, new to the district, who parted with a large cheque for a top-grade .222 rifle complete with telescopic sight, scope-mounted lamp, leather case and enough expensive cartridges to have decimated the fox and roe-deer populations of southern Scotland. He departed, staggering slightly under the weight of his purchases. I wished him luck, given which he might breed another generation of rich and acquisitive shooters.

The shop was empty again when a solidly built man paused at the door, looked both ways around the Square and then made up his mind to come inside. My first impression was that he had the face of a cartoon character, stereotypical of the unthinking hard man. I prepared myself for another rush of business but it appeared that my first impression was the correct one.

Without preamble, he came up close, grabbed me by the tie and pulled me halfway across the counter.

'I've a bone to pick with you,' he said, in a voice which rumbled deep in his chest.

Between nerves and the pressure on my throat, clear speech was not easy. 'Wok?' I said. By good luck the CB radio was alive and close to my hand. Without losing eye-contact I fumbled one-handed for a second until I found the TRANSMIT key.

'You ken damned fine what,' he retorted. His accent came from somewhere within thirty miles of Glasgow, and not from one of the better neighbourhoods. 'You've been sticking your damn nose in where it's not wanted.' I hoped that Janet was listening and that she would have the sense both to tape the conversation and to phone the police. 'You manked up an easy wee pochle, got Doug catched and now you've been trying to fix for Madam Fancypants to point them my way.'

'Let go of me,' I squawked as loudly and as clearly as I could, hoping that the urgency of my position would communicate itself to Janet. At the same time my mind surprised me by thinking clearly and dispassionately that for the man to know as much as he did, Mrs Ritson-Jones had been either treacherous or in deep trouble.

'Let bloody go of you?' He gave me a shake by the tie which for a moment cut off my air altogether. 'And have you grab for one of these guns? That'll be the day. I'll stiffen you first. Other way round, Jimmy. We lost most of our cash and our only shooter in that barn. I'll give you three guesses whose turn it is to come across. When I've got the tools of my trade again I can soon be back in funds. First, reach out slowly and open the till.'

The money in the cash register was unimportant, being largely in the form of cheques which would be valueless to him and could at a pinch be replaced; but if I let a violent criminal walk out of the shop with one or more of our stock of handguns, our days as registered dealers would be numbered. And at the same time my chances of being left alive and undamaged would be slim . . .

Evidently, he regarded me as no kind of threat. But beside the cash register lay a G.10 pistol. It was only an air pistol but it was a more or less faithful copy of a semi-automatic pistol – and, if it failed to deceive, it was heavy enough to deliver a satisfactory whack across the thickest skull.

I was just preparing for a desperate effort when I heard, faintly through the concrete, the sound of feet clattering in haste down the stair from the flat above.

The man detected some shift in my attitude and the ever ready antennae of the hunted gave a twitch. His eyes roamed and I saw them notice the pistol beside the cash register. He hauled so that my feet almost left the floor. 'Don't even think of it,' he grunted.

For a second or two there was nothing I could do but endure. Interruption was on the way. Whether it would amount to rescue was uncertain, but at least it would confuse a situation which was too simple for my liking.

The shop door burst open, setting the bell jangling. Janet entered, still wrapped in her overall but incongruously carrying her second-best handbag. There was no sign of any police back-up, but Janet herself in her fury was as swift and unstoppable as a whirlwind.

The man turned to face her without releasing my tie.

Janet crossed the floor in a quick pitterpat, swinging her handbag overhead as she came. It moved ponderously, as though she had paused to fill it with sand. The man let go of my tie at last and raised his hands to ward off a blow to the head, but Janet reversed her swing and the handbag arrived in a vicious underarm blow to the man's crotch. He dropped his hands but the weighted bag brushed through them – breaking a thumb in the process as I later learned – and almost lifted him off the floor.

The man landed on his knees. He had turned very white, his tongue protruded and I think that his eyes were crossed. He was exhaling a single endless breath until I thought that he must shrivel away like a balloon. I had a certain sympathy for him. My own testicles may have descended many years earlier but at the sight and sound of that blow they tried to crawl back up again. He was perfectly presented for the unnecessary *coup de grâce* that followed – a return overhand swing to the top of his head which put him down and clean out.

Janet threw down her bag with a heavy thump and came at me like a mad woman. I was loosening my tie in preparation for taking several long breaths, but she grabbed my tie again and pulled me half across the counter much as the man had done. She snatched the Nitrolingual spray from my pocket, jerked open my mouth – she seemed to have been gifted suddenly with a dozen pairs of hands – and shot a long blast of spray, mostly into my mouth.

Only then did she get around to asking me whether I was all right.

At last I managed to loosen my tie. 'Perfectly,' I croaked, with as much dignity as I could manage considering that I was still half choked and disarranged.

'You're sure?'

I nodded and drew in a dozen deep breaths before trying to speak again. 'Certain,' I said. It was a lie, but a white one.

'Good. Cops?' She seemed to be living at high speed.

'Have to,' I said. 'Watch what you say.' Her verbal shorthand was catching.

She leaped at the phone and informed the police, in about six words, that somebody whom they very much wanted was awaiting collection.

The police, in the person of a disbelieving constable, had only to cross the Square, and arrived within a minute or two. The ambulance summoned by the suddenly persuaded officer took longer, dead-heating with reinforcements which included Inspector Ian Fellowes, Keith's son-in-law.

My conscious but still groaning attacker was lifted into the ambulance under the eyes of the crowd. (In the quiet town of Newton Lauder, seven or eight curious bystanders constitute a crowd.) Two officers travelled in the ambulance, in case the man recovered consciousness and either fought to escape or wanted to make a statement. The other three, including Ian Fellowes, remained behind, asking questions and making notes.

We had had time to cool down and to arrive at an outline agreement before the first officer turned up, but our one attempt to phone Ralph Enterkin had come up against the impassable barrier of his secretary/receptionist. In our statements to the police, rather than upset whatever delicate negotiations the solicitor might be conducting, we confined ourselves to the man's attack on me, his demand for money and firearms, my use of the CB radio to alert Janet and her gallop to the rescue.

A police surgeon, who turned out to be my own doctor, was summoned to examine the marks on my neck. He also listened to my heart and pronounced it none the worse for the exercise. He then followed up the ambulance to the hospital, ready to record for purposes of any future litigation whatever damage the unfortunate gentleman might have suffered at the hands of my violent spouse. Ian was inclined to pooh-

pooh the idea of a successful lawsuit but, as I pointed out to Janet when the police at last left us to ourselves, Ian had not witnessed the first blow struck.

'Believe me,' I said, 'I'm thoroughly behind you and duly grateful. You performed perfectly, and far better than I had any right to expect. But if he did care to take us to court and argue that you used greater force than was strictly necessary, we might have a job proving that the whack over the less delicate organ – his head – wouldn't have been enough on its own.'

Janet, in the letdown after her adrenalin high, was inclined to be tearful. She picked up what had once been a favourite and expensive handbag and studied the burst stitches. I saw that she had tipped a couple of boxes of twelve-bore cartridges into it, to add their considerable weight – a trick which, she told me later, Molly Calder had taught her. 'The smack on his head wouldn't have been so effective if I hadn't hit him first in the nuts,' she pointed out. 'He won't really sue me, will he?'

'I don't suppose so,' I said reassuringly. 'A claim that "She hit me with her handbag" would sound so daft that any man would hesitate to try it on a jury, let alone a man who depends on a reputation for toughness for his living. We don't have to say anything about the cartridges. He may take a different view if it turns out that you've wrecked his future sex-life. But if the need should ever arise, don't hesitate to do it again and harder. Don't let the thought of the occasional lawsuit put you off. And now' – I looked at my watch – 'we're halfway through our usual lunch-break.'

'I'll go and make something.'

I was about to offer to buy her a proper lunch in the hotel when the CB radio, which had been sitting silent and forgotten on the counter, suddenly came to life.

'Mr James,' it said. 'Mr James. Somebody. Anybody.

124

Can you hear me?' The voice could have been a woman's or a boy's, or possibly a high-pitched man's, but there was something about its timbre that made the hairs rise on my neck.

The faint hiss of the carrier wave stopped. I depressed the button to transmit and said, 'This is Wallace James. I can hear you. Who's there? Over.'

'Joanna Ritson-Jones.' Her voice was faint and yet strained, as though she had to shout to make herself heard. I thought that her battery might be running out. 'You have to come and help me.'

'Where are you?'

'In the woods, near your partner's house. I'm in awful trouble and I don't know how much more I can take. Come quickly. No police. Oh God! Hurry!' I thought that she was talking through tears and I was sure of it when her message ended on a wail.

Janet grabbed the CB radio. 'What's wrong?' she asked. We waited. There was no answer. 'How do we find you? Never mind. We're coming,' she told it. 'Come on.' She hauled me towards the door. I could only be thankful that for once somebody had grabbed me by the hand instead of the tie.

'It could be a trap,' I said.

'How? Both the men are locked up.'

'There's still a blackmailer plus God alone knows who else on the loose,' I pointed out. 'Offhand I can imagine several different people wanting to close her mouth or ours.'

Janet thought swiftly. 'Bring a gun,' she said. 'You have permission to carry a gun in Belcast Woods and what's one more charge of excessive violence among so many?'

Rather than argue, I unlocked the security wire and took a gun from the rack. 'Bring the radio,' I said. 'We may need it if we can't find her straight away.'

I had chosen a folding single-barrel twelve-bore which went under my jacket, more or less, and attracted no attention as I crossed the few yards of the Square to our car. Janet locked the shop and followed. Long-standing habit reasserted itself and I took the driver's seat.

An artic was trying to pass between two vans but an old lady had somehow jammed her Mini into the tangle. We had to wait. 'Are you all right?' Janet asked again.

'Fine. I already told you.'

'To drive, I mean.'

I assured her that I was quite calm and competent and had even come through my recent experiences without a trace of angina.

'Good. We're on the way,' she said into the radio.

'Where's your handbag?' I asked her.

'I left it on the counter. Well, the stitching was split.'

'Hellfire!' I said.

'It's all right. I'll take it to the saddler tomorrow.'

A channel opened up and I bullied our way through to the tune of horns. We picked up speed as we neared open country. 'That's just great,' I said. 'I have a gun but I was counting on the cartridges in your bag.'

'Nobody would know that it wasn't loaded,' she pointed out.

'Better and better. So they decide that they may as well shoot first. An empty gun puts the holder in more danger than no gun at all.'

'Oh.' The thought seemed to be both new and unwelcome. 'Perhaps we'd better be careful.'

'Believe me, I already had that in mind,' I told her.

Once on the open road, I wound the car up to a speed which it had never attained before. For once, Janet made no protest and I could even feel her willing me on. Almost immediately, I was slowing to turn off.

Belcast Woods are made up of a tract of mixed wood-

126

land, much of it coniferous plantation of varying ages, parts of which are harvested and replanted in due course, mingled with older, natural growths of pine and silver birch, the whole lying between Briesland House and the old town road. The area is much favoured by locals for rambles or picnics and by children for whatever adventures their fertile imaginations can generate, but only lovers and dedicated birdwatchers ever penetrate much beyond the mixed woodland which fronts on the road.

The tracks into the woods change with the operations of the foresters but at that time there was only one entry accessible by car. We passed the mouth of Keith's by-road and turned off into a ride which was now a year old. Level enough, it was developing a grassy surface which would be hell in wet weather but which was easy driving in the dry conditions.

'Shall I try to find out exactly where she is?' Janet asked, lifting the radio.

I was not keen to broadcast our arrival. 'She'd have told us if she was hidden,' I said. 'Let's take a look first.'

The ride rose, fell and occasionally made a slight change of direction but progressed generally westward. The mixed woodland gave way to the conifers. The sweet smell of resin was all around us. We looked along every firebreak that we crossed. Briesland House was almost in sight before we saw, up ahead, the motor caravan from the barn.

'The police must have accepted Mrs Ritson-Jones's story about intending to buy it,' I said.

Janet let out a snort. 'They didn't seem to believe a bloody word we told them,' she said, 'and then they go and swallow some tale that that trollop spins them. Wait until I see Ian!'

I stopped the car while we were still a hundred yards

off. Nothing moved except a kestrel, hovering in its search for small rodents. The caravan looked deserted. It had only halted where a drainage ditch prevented further progress and it was parked in the shelter of a stand of firs, with a step at the door, a bucket under the waste pipe and a small toilet tent nearby. When I opened my door I could hear birdsong. It was a cosy scene which could have passed for the campsite of a family on holiday, but my imagination, triggered by the ominous phone-call, was working overtime.

We got out of the car. I held the shotgun at the ready, but I was prepared to throw it down in a hurry if anybody should appear whose armament might be loaded. I was also prepared to take off like a sprinter for the nearest trees and let my heart take its chance.

The walk seemed to take for ever but nobody ambushed us from the trees. A small flock of pigeon swept over the treetops, scattering when they saw me. Higher, rooks were circling, well above shot. A rabbit bolted suddenly from almost underfoot, its white scut bobbing away into the trees, and my heart performed the sort of gyration against which my doctor had warned me.

As we got closer to the caravan, I could see that a rough patch of felt had been stuck over the hole I had made in the roof. Curtains were drawn over the windows. The trees stifled any breeze and all was still except that I thought that there were sounds inside the van, faint sounds, unnatural sounds.

Whatever was waiting would not go away. I would have to jerk the door of the van open and hope that no bogey was waiting to pounce. I brought the useless shotgun to the ready.

As the door slid back, we had a glimpse of the interior. Then Janet, who had been on my heels as we approached, pushed past me, leaped inside and slid the door closed behind her. I was left to wait outside on the grass with a photographic image in my mind of a female figure, which I took to be that of Mrs Ritson-Jones, lying on the restricted floorspace between the bunks. I was in no doubt that she had been brutally abused. A florid collection of welts and bruises was in full view, because most of her clothing, now ripped to shreds, was tossed on the bunks. Her wrists and ankles and also her knees and elbows were tied so tightly that the cord was embedded into the skin. A CB radio rather like our own lay near her whitened hand, which explained the straining of her voice. She would have had to shout.

I sat on the step and did some more thinking. The unexpected knowledge shown by my earlier visitor was also explained. I could hear soothing noises from inside the caravan and guessed that compassion had overcome any old grudges, or else Janet was heaping biblical coals of fire on Mrs Ritson-Jones's head.

After some ten minutes the door slid open a crack. 'Are you all right?' Janet asked. It had become her standard greeting.

'Perfectly,' I said. I had become so used to the exchange that I would probably have made the same answer unthinkingly from my deathbed.

'Take a squirt of your spray anyway,' she said, 'and then go back to the car.' The caravan door slid shut again.

I trudged back to the car. As I entered the driver's seat I heard the motor caravan's engine start. It moved towards me and stopped door-to-door. Janet's head came out. 'Follow along after us,' she said. Nobody else was to be seen. Mrs Ritson-Jones, presumably, was on one of the bunks. Janet drove off. The bucket, the step and the toilet tent were still where they had been but it was no part of my duties to pick them up, especially when I remembered that the entire set-up was probably stolen. I followed the lurching caravan back to the road and towards Newton Lauder.

In the outskirts of the town they stopped and to judge from the jerking of Janet's head there was an argument. Then the motor caravan moved on again and came to rest in the Square in the nearest available parking slot to the shop. Janet got out and helped Mrs Ritson-Jones, who was now washed clean of blood and decently shrouded in a tweed coat but walking only with difficulty, over to our front door.

The Square was busy now. It took me a minute or two to find and squeeze into a parking space which was a little further off – a space which had been left vacant because the cars on either side had encroached on the dividing line. I followed the others at a slower pace, reminding myself firmly that my days of hurrying upstairs were behind me.

Mrs Ritson-Jones was draped along our couch, wrapped in my favourite dressing gown and still managing to look almost glamorous, while Janet attempted to improve on her earlier and hasty attempts at first aid.

'What are we doing here?' I asked. 'I would have thought that the hospital—'

'I am not going National Health,' Mrs Ritson-Jones said firmly, lisping through swollen lips. (Janet looked up and winked.) 'If you can wait around long enough they do a good job on your injuries, but they don't worry too much about what scars they leave. My father may have cut off my allowance but he'll pay for a good cosmetic surgeon.' She gave a bitter laugh but was careful not to smile. 'He knows that if I lose my looks he'd be stuck with me for ever.'

'—or the police—' I struggled on.

'Definitely no police. Not yet.'

'Then perhaps Mr Enterkin—'

'Now you're coming to the boil,' Mrs Ritson-Jones said more approvingly. She shut her mouth, flinching while Janet swabbed round her lips, but for the moment I had offered all my best suggestions. 'I had an appointment to see him this afternoon,' she said when Janet had moved on, 'and now I've got rather more to trade.'

'If you're including the former partner of Doug Waller and yourself,' I said, 'you're too late. I presume that he beat you until you told him who had given Mr Waller to the cops?'

'I'm sorry about that,' she said, for once sounding almost sincere. 'I thought I could stand pain but I find that I can't, not on the scale that that imaginative bastard can inflict it.' She shivered. 'He said he was going to come back and . . . dispose of me. How did you know?'

'He came here,' I told her, 'but Janet whacked him in the goolies with her handbag and he's in custody now. So don't rely too heavily on him as a bargaining counter.'

'I just may have a little more than that to bargain with,' Mrs Ritson-Jones said slowly.

'I wish you'd keep still,' Janet said. 'Wal, it's time you went to open the shop.'

'What about lunch?' I asked.

'No time for that just now.'

'How hard did she whack him?' Mrs Ritson-Jones asked me.

I decided to throw her a little comfort. 'With all her might,' I said. 'And her handbag was weighted.'

This time, although it clearly hurt her mouth, Mrs Ritson-Jones could not help smiling.

I put up a note in the shop's door and went over to the hotel for a late lunch.

EIGHT

No doubt the waves from all this activity continued to agitate the legal waters, but our quiet backwater remained remarkably undisturbed. Ralph Enterkin whisked Mrs Ritson-Jones away – into private medical care, I was led to believe. He was also present when the police sought our further statements, although nothing asked or answered seemed to cause him any concern. We let it be thought that the man had been after money and one or more guns, and left it there. The police, who profoundly dislike firearms in any hands but their own, were approving of Janet's violence while reserving the right to perform a volte-face if they or the procurator fiscal should happen to feel so inclined.

After that, all went quiet and stayed the same. Janet seemed disinclined to discuss her changed attitude to her old enemy.

Even the trout were sluggish. Johnson Laing and I persuaded Janet, who was coming round to the idea that fishing was a suitably therapeutic activity, to drive us to Moorfoot Loch. Along with a dozen other ticket-holders we pursued the rainbow stockies for an hour with no return although one or two splashy rises could be seen to terrestrial insects dancing out from the shore. Even various nymphs twitched temptingly near the bottom failed to produce any reaction. But I did feel the occasional tug at a Greenwell's Glory, so we switched to a favourite of mine, a wingless Greenwell tied with a parachute hackle and cast from the shore almost into the mouths of the few rising fish. The result was that we soon had our limit, to the surprise and indignation of those present.

(Later, as word went round, there began a steady trickle of orders to the shop for what some humorist christened Wal's Wonder. I charged over the odds for it on the grounds that the parachute hackle took longer to tie than the regular version, although with practice I found that I could turn one out every few minutes. If the fish continued to take my Wonder while refusing all else, nobody was being robbed.)

As we returned towards home, near the junction where the road from Moorfoot Loch joined the main road we came across a rusty and travel-stained Cavalier, facing towards Newton Lauder but firmly ditched. The driver, who was alone, was still seated at the wheel and as we came near he made a forceful if hopeless attempt to drive his car back onto the road. There was no other traffic in sight.

Janet pulled up in front of the other car and opened her door. 'I'll ask him if he wants us to send him help,' she said.

'My tow-rope should still be in the back if it's wanted,' I said.

'Right.' Janet walked back. A moment later I heard her calling to me.

'Sit tight,' I told Johnson. 'No point all of us getting heated.'

Janet met me halfway. 'See who it is?' she said. 'And he's well over the limit.'

The driver was swaying in his seat and blinking into space. His face, which looked unnaturally white, was faintly familiar but it took me a few seconds to place it. 'Dennis Pratt,' I said to Janet. 'One of the men who

133

accused Jim Waterhouse of poisoning sparrowhawks.'

'That's the man,' she said. 'We'll have to be quick or the police will be along.'

'Do we really care?' I asked her. 'I'd rather wait around and enjoy a good laugh.'

'Trust me,' she said. 'Play it my way. We don't have time for debate. Get Johnson to come and sit in Pratt's car. Quickly. Can you manage to put on the tow-rope without over-exerting yourself?'

When Janet takes the bit between her teeth I find it best to let her have her head. 'I'll go canny,' I said.

'Take your time.'

I went back to our car. 'The driver's pissed out of his skull,' I told Johnson. 'We're going to try to save his bacon. Would you go and sit in his driving seat while we try to tow it out? He can sit here.'

Johnson smiled and opened his door. 'The idiot doesn't deserve friends like you. But I feel euphoric after the fresh air, sunshine, fishing and making those other twits turn green with envy, so I'll go along with you without calling the fuzz.'

'Be patient,' I said. 'This may take a little time.'

Janet was persuading Dennis Pratt out of his car. He managed to walk fairly steadily to ours and settled in a back seat. He was an ill-proportioned man and his suit had evidently been tailor-made for him. At some point he seemed to have peed on his suede shoes. Johnson took his place and Janet sat beside Pratt in the back of our car.

As I got out the tow-rope and fitted it, taking my time as instructed, I could hear most of what was said between Janet and Pratt. Janet started by pointing out what Pratt must have known well, that he was in dire trouble.

'Niece's wedding,' he said thickly. 'Won't happen again, I swear. Help me, please.'

134

Janet's voice took on the firm metallic tone that she uses whenever she wants to be sure that I am not just pretending to listen. 'You are going to answer some questions,' she said. 'If the police happen along before you've satisfied me with your answers, we'll hand you over. But if you're a good boy...'

'What in your 'pinion constipates being a good boy?' he asked.

'Telling me what I want to know.'

'What then?'

'Then maybe you were a passenger.'

'Tha's blackmail.'

'True,' Janet said.

There was a pause while Pratt's anaesthetized mind struggled to catch up. 'What you want to know?' he asked at last.

It was Janet's turn to pause. The opening had presented itself so suddenly that her thoughts were still in disarray. 'I won't even ask you whether the charges against Jim Waterhouse were trumped up. That goes without saying. And you a respected member of the RSPB! What's more,' she added as Pratt made a strangled sound of protest, 'if you waste time arguing about it, the police will come by before you've managed to satisfy me. Or, if not, I'll call them myself.

'You were a friend of Mr Berry. Right?'

Through the rear window I saw Pratt's head nodding. 'Good friend,' he said. 'Only one he'd got, really. Nobody loved him.'

'Not even his wife?' Janet asked quickly. I wondered if she was picturing Mrs Berry pushing her husband into the river.

'Wives don't count, not that sort of way.'

'Did Ken Berry put you up to framing Jim Waterhouse?'

Dennis Pratt might be 'drink taken' but he was still

too cautious either to make an admission or to call Janet's bluff. 'He might have,' he said at last.

'I'll take that as a yes. Now, here's the big question,' Janet said. 'This could be what decides whether you go home or into the slammer. Colonel McInsch is being blackmailed by a journalist. Did you tip the journalist off?'

'No!' Pratt's squawk of indignation sounded genuine.

'I think I see a blue lamp flashing in the distance,' Janet said. I looked in both directions but saw no such thing.

'It wasn't me,' Pratt said desperately. 'That was Gordon Milne, passing on what was going round locally. Told him not to. But there must've been something in it. Can't blackmail a man over nothing. Lousy trick all the same.'

'Worse than faking evidence against Jim Waterhouse?'

''ccording to Gordon Milne, Waterhouse really was poisoning sparrowhawks.'

'And that would have made it all right?'

'Seemed all right at the time.' Pratt spoke through an enormous yawn.

Janet decided that debating either facts or ethics with a bigoted drunk would be a waste of limited time. 'Was . . . is . . . Colonel McInsch being blackmailed about the old incident of his evidence for Jim Waterhouse? Or the death of Mr Berry?'

'It wasn't about Ken Berry,' Pratt said sleepily. 'It started before that. Gordon met some folk who'd seen something, not quite what the Colonel told the sheriff. McInsch and the pup were fishing right enough on the day the case was about. They were on McInsch's bit of the river but Waterhouse wasn't with 'em, morning or afternoon.

'Gordon was only trying to sell the story, get a bit of

money for the tip-off, but, next thing, he was in for a share of what the Colonel would cough up.'

'It didn't occur to him to tell the police, or even the Colonel?' Janet asked sternly.

'Too late for that. There was some hard man got hold of him, told him to keep his trap shut or else. Honest to God, 's all I know.'

'These witnesses. Who were they?'

No answer.

'Those were the Parkers, weren't they? Hey!' Janet said. 'Wake up! I haven't finished with you.'

But even from outside the car I could hear Pratt beginning to snore. Janet got out and took several breaths of fresh air. 'Let's see if we can pull the gowk's car out of the ditch and get him home. And may the devil take him for his own!'

I was feeling more confident in my health as each day went by. Janet printed up a notice which read 'Overconfidence may seriously damage your health' and pinned it to the inside of the front door. I avoided physical effort or mental stress whenever I could, but I was quite happy to resume doing my share of the shop-work. This pleased Keith, who was thus freed to get on with the gun repairs at home or, when that work was up to date, to take a dog and a gun and go rabbiting or lie in wait for the magpies and carrion crows which haunted our shoot in the hope of easy pickings at other birds' eggs or chicks.

Our wives, however, while relieved at my recovery soon became less than happy at my devotion to the shop. They had always been close friends and enjoyed each other's company on shopping sprees or in doing their share of shop duty together. But while Keith was out and about and I was in the shop, and often alone for long periods, it was considered necessary for one

137

of them to be monitoring me by way of the CB radio. This put a brake on their joint outings and they missed both each other's company and the constantly changing faces that entered the shop. Chatterboxes the pair of them, they were suffering withdrawal symptoms. Soon they were almost begging me, for God's sake, to go fishing or else.

Jim Waterhouse, when I phoned him, sounded embarrassed. 'I telled the Colonel I'd given you my invite,' he said, 'but he's no' keen to let you at the salmon at a', though I canno' think why. It's no' as though he was fishing the beats hissel'.'

'We're not after the salmon,' I reminded him. 'Trout will do.'

Jim, though he very much enjoyed a grilled trout with almonds, was a shooting man through and through and had no great opinion of any fish as a quarry that ran to less than six or seven pounds. 'They wee thingies? You're daft, man.'

'Any fool can let a gaudy fly drift across a pool and annoy a salmon into snapping at it,' I retorted. 'Trout are picky eaters and they know what their natural food looks like, where it should be and how it would behave. You have to put the right thing in the right place in the right way. That takes skill. I enjoy a day or two at the salmon now and again, but mostly I'd just as soon fish for trout any day of the week. Anyway,' I added, remembering suddenly, 'we're both cardiac patients. We're not supposed to lift heavy weights.'

'That's different,' Jim said. 'I don't suppose the Colonel will give a damn about a few finnock. When are you coming?'

'Tomorrow?' I suggested.

'The morn will be fine. Come to the house.'

Johnson Laing's nephew-in-law was not only at home from his oil rig but had swept our usual driver away on an umpteenth honeymoon – which, we were assured in case we should take her defection personally, was his habit when returning from offshore with money in his pocket. Keith, who was going away on some ploy of his own, dropped us at Jim's house, promising that somebody unspecified would come back for us in the late afternoon.

Jim lived with his wife in a modest but respectable house served by its own short spur from the drive up to McInsch House. Backed by open woodland, it faced obliquely across the main drive and a tree-dotted stretch of parkland to part of a large backwater left behind some twenty years earlier on the last of the many occasions when the river had changed its course and so added to the argument and dissension between the landowners. The main stream was now on the far side of a narrow wooded island. Beyond, on the Castle Berrys side of the river, the scenery changed from park to farmland and became a landscape of small to medium-sized fields divided by hedgerows. It was a charmingly picturesque scene, old fashioned almost to the point of being quaint and, to be frank, far more attractive than the view enjoyed by the Big House.

Dutifully, we knocked at the door to report our presence, then donned our waders and firmly resisted Jim's efforts to hale us indoors for a dram, although we did accept his wife's invitation to eat our lunchtime sandwiches in their kitchen.

The backwater was reputed to be alive with brown trout, some of them of notable size, but the fishing was extremely difficult by virtue of the very weed growth which gave them food and shelter. The breeze had come round to the north, there was an unseasonable chill in the air and most of the fish were feeding deep. Johnson gathered a brace of three-quarter pounders by casting one of my weighted red shrimps into the holes in the weed, while I collected five, mostly larger, trout by dapping a fly over those same holes but at the expense of losing as many hooks to the aquatic jungle. A quick strike and lift was needed to get each taker onto the surface and over the weed before it could entangle itself in the safety of the roots.

When hunger began to outweigh the avarice of the hunter, we returned to Jim's house. Jim was away by then, collecting a load of pheasant poults from the game farm, but Mrs Waterhouse welcomed us into her kitchen and was so liberal with a home-made meat and vegetable soup that we had little appetite for sandwiches. I noticed Jim's salmon rod, assembled with taped joints and ready for immediate use if a run of fish should begin, hung neatly along a row of hooks in the hall.

Mrs Waterhouse was a cheerful woman. She had a cackling laugh, but much could be forgiven her because she was kind hearted, a talented cook, still pretty and had a ready wit. We ate, she kept us chuckling with mildly scandalous stories from the early days of some of the local bigwigs, only sobering when Johnson, curious as ever, dragged the late Mr Berry into the conversation.

'I never could thole that man,' she said reluctantly. 'What's more, I'm as sure as I can be that he was at the back of it, the time my Jim was taken up for poisoning hawks, as if Jim would do sic a thing. Those twa that spoke up agin him were cronies of Mr Berry and if he didn't put them up to it I know for a fact that he was behind those rumours about the Colonel having lied himself hoarse to get Jim let off. The same way that the tales themselves travel round, so does mention of who told who. You know what I mean? "So-and-so says..." It was just that way, and when the names mentioned are every one of them as thick as thieves with one man, well, I ken what to think.' She sighed.

'If I was asked to swear on the Bible that I was sorry he was dead, well, I couldn't do it and that's all there is about it.'

'I wouldn't expect you to,' I said. 'Tell me, did you ever have a journalist poking around, looking for a story?'

'Aye, I did. There was a mannie here just after my Jim stood trial. He tried to use Mr Berry's name to get me to say that the Colonel wasn't here that day at all. He'd already been at Mrs Watson, the housekeeper, but she sent him away with a flea in his ear. Anyway, what would I know about the Colonel's comings and goings? I told him, if he wanted to dig in the dirt he should go and speak to those Nosy Parkers.'

'The Parkers?' I said. 'They're around here almost every day, I hear. Weren't they here the day that Mr Berry drowned?'

'I'm sure I wouldn't know about that,' Mrs Waterhouse said. I thought that her manner was less easy.

'But you were looking out,' I said. 'Jim said that you saw most of it from the sitting-room window.'

'I didno' see that much,' she said. 'Just when I went to the door, I saw the Colonel pulling him out onto the rocky point below the backwater and trying to get him breathing again.' Mrs Waterhouse pulled herself up and looked towards a stack of laundry awaiting her iron. 'But I'm keeping you from the fishing.'

We took the hint. I paused on the doorstep and looked towards the tip of the island. A small group of trees hid the rocks. Thinking back, they would already have been in leaf when Kenneth Berry died. It was not very significant. Mrs Waterhouse could have walked a few yards either way without seeing any need to mention the fact.

The cold northerly breeze, funnelling down the valley roughly from the direction of the barn where I had

141

spiked the motor caravan, began to blow more strongly. Any hatch of insects soon ceased and as the surface of the water cooled all the trout were feeding deep. Not even a dapped Mayfly would draw them to the surface.

The effort of nymphing the bottom with an artificial bloodworm through that weed palled on me by mid-afternoon. We decided to move to the river which, although less of a favourite with trout, would be easier by far to fish. There was no way onto the island between the backwater and the mainstream without swimming or the use of a boat. Johnson elected to walk upstream to where, above the top of the island, the water bustled between wooded banks into the head of a long, slow pool, so I went downstream by way of the drive. Jim's returning pick-up passed me and he gave me a wave.

The backwater returned to the main river at the point where an outcrop of rock had forced the river to make a sudden bend in its original course. I picked my way over an uneven rocky surface. In the distance, and roughly opposite the small headland from which I understood Ken Berry to have made his fatal plunge, I could see Johnson casting under the branches of some sycamores in search of the odd fish that might be waiting for wind-blown insects. My own position was less propitious. I had seen a salmon arch out of the water and re-enter with a splash and where one had leaped there would be a dozen below. If one of them gave a peevish or playful snatch at my fly, I could make an enemy of the Colonel.

I changed my spool for one with a fast-sinking line and tied on a weighted imitation of a cased caddis larva. That, trundling along the sandy bottom, should not attract the attention of a salmon but there might be a trout lying in wait for just such a titbit being swept

142

down from the shallows just above the place where Johnson was now striving to disentangle his line from the branches overhead.

Where I stood, the river was little more than thirty yards wide and, with the wind behind me, I had to be careful not to over-cast and become entangled in the reeds and gorse which were waiting for me on the far bank. I managed to drop my lure just short of trouble.

My first cast came back with only a couple of twitches that might have been no more than the hook snagging bottom. I lengthened line by another yard and cast again at a more downstream angle, got a firm pull and lifted the rod; and as line was ripped off the reel I knew immediately that I was into a salmon.

'Stay cool,' I told my beating heart. And, 'Get rid of him quickly before the Colonel shows up,' I told myself. I let line run free in the hope that he could shake out the hook. When that failed, I lowered the rod and hauled. My leader should have snapped, but thin nylon, unkinked and properly tied, can often take far more than its nominal breaking strain. He came round and charged back upstream.

The fish fought grimly without ever showing itself at the surface. There were no spectacular leaps, just powerful runs that felt as though I was holding a submarine by its cable. Several times the fish seemed to tire but each time it found new energy and was off again.

After five or six minutes of unremitting battle I could feel that the rushes were less frequent, less long and less powerful. I recovered line steadily. A swirl showed where the fish was being drawn into shallower water. Then, quite suddenly, he was on his side at the surface. Not a salmon, not even a sea trout, but a wild brown trout, one of those rare fish that have avoided anglers and other predators and grown to specimen size, in splendid condition with brilliant spots, hooked firmly in the scissors of the jaw.

'That is some fish,' said a voice behind me. 'If I ever land one like that, I'll die happy. Not immediately, I hasten to add.'

Half expecting to see Colonel McInsch, I glanced over my shoulder. Johnson Laing was approaching carefully over the smooth rocks.

'Five and a half pounds if not six, and fighting fit. What are you doing here?' I asked him.

'I wasn't doing any good up there. Too many trees, too close. By the time I'd lost a whole swarm of flies I knew that I'd have to catch a basketful of trout to recover the cost.'

'If you apply standards of cost effectiveness to your fishing,' I said absently, 'you'll quit. Since you're here, get my camera out of my fishing bag. We'll have a record of this one.' I had the fish over the net at last.

'You're not going to keep him?' Johnson said wistfully.

'No.' Others think me mad, but I have strong ethical objection to catch-and-release. Something in me rebels at the idea of putting a fellow creature through pain and fear just for the thrill of the struggle. Although fish have little memory of pain – one may catch the same fish again on the same fly a few minutes later – it seems to me to be treating them as toys. I fish for pleasure but I expect to eat my catch or to give it to somebody else who will appreciate it. But this one was special. For no good reason, I felt that he deserved a chance to grow still larger. Besides, extra-large trout never retain a good flavour. I held the fish in my carefully wetted hands while Johnson opened my bag and photographed the pair of us from every angle. Then I clipped the barb off the hook and the big trout was free. I rocked him in the water until he had recovered. He stirred, kicked and was gone.

Johnson doffed his tweed cap to the departing swirl. 'Are you ready to pack up now? We could phone for our lift.'

'One or two last casts . . .' I said wistfully. A single success in difficult conditions always brings with it the feeling that 'this time I've really cracked it'. The sun had come out and I was warm after the exercise. My chest was not delivering any warning aches.

'I'm in no hurry,' Johnson seated himself carefully on a hump of rock.

I tied on a new and more heavily weighted cased caddis, took a few paces downstream and cast warily, mindful of Johnson's position almost under my backcast. My line settled on the water, vanished and came round more slowly and in fits and starts, evidently scraping over the bottom. Then it halted and resisted me. The faint vibration was the current strumming the taut line, not the thrashing of a fish. I decided that I was probably into a submerged snag. I was quite prepared to break my leader – I make my cased caddis lures from sections of ballpoint pen innards coated with glue and rolled in sand, and they are the most expendable of all my flies – but when I gave a strong pull it came heavily, as though I had hooked into a ball of weed.

'An old tyre?' Johnson suggested from behind me.

'Not as heavy as that,' I said. 'Maybe a small branch from a tree.' Line was coming in more easily now. But when my nylon leader came to the surface, incredibly, instead of my caddis I seemed to have acquired a Jock Scott salmon fly.

My first thought was that if the Colonel happened along I would never be able to convince him that I had not been after his salmon. My second and equally daft thought was that some impish scuba-diver had changed my fly in order to queer my pitch with the Colonel. There seemed to be no other explanation.

As I pulled in my leader, however, I realized that

my caddis was still in place although hidden under the larger fly, that the Jock Scott was on another line which my hook had gathered and that a lead weight of about one ounce had somehow become attached to the pair.

This made no sense at all.

I began to pull the other line in, hand over hand. What seemed to be about ten feet of eighteen-pound nylon leader gave way to salmon line, about 12 on the AFTM scale, which began to fall in loops and whorls around my feet as I hauled it in.

Johnson had come to stand beside me. 'What now?' he said.

'We'll see,' I told him.

After about thirty metres, the green fly-line ended, joined by a needle knot to the backing. The braided backing, thin but very strong, seemed to go on for ever.

'Somebody lost the end of the line off his reel?' Johnson suggested. 'Or dropped the whole reel?'

'Or the whole gubbins including the rod,' I said.

'You're not supposed to be doing any sustained work.' Johnson took the line out of my hands and resumed the hauling in.

'Nor are you,' I pointed out.

'So we share it. My turn!'

Admitting to myself that I was slightly breathless, I took a seat where Johnson had been sitting, wound in the rest of my own line and hooked the fly into the false ring. 'A rod can be lost easily enough,' I said, 'if a fish takes the fly while the angler's laid his rod down for a moment. More often from a boat than the bank.'

'There was no sign of a fish.'

I got up and dug among the coils of line until I found the gaudy fly. The acidity in a fish's mouth soon dissolves the point of a hook. The twin hooks were intact except that the barbs had been squeezed flat with pliers. 'Barbless,' I said. 'Somebody practised catch-and-release, or at least he wanted to be able to let the fish get away with the least possible damage if he hooked one that was colouring up for spawning.'

'Is that so?' Johnson asked uncomprehendingly. He was an experienced trout-fisher but his acquaintance with salmon was of the slightest. 'Here it comes,' he added.

Tip first, a salmon rod followed the line out of the water. It was a quality rod, taped at the joints. The tip was broken but the backing line held the parts together. I took it from Johnson and began to wind the line back onto the reel before the loose coils on the ground could get into a hopeless tangle. Johnson looked anxious. 'Aren't you offending against one of the cardinal principles of detection?' he asked.

'It can't have been Ken Berry's rod,' I pointed out in extenuation. 'His was found on the bank. Or was that report false?'

'No. At least, they found a rod on the bank.'

'There you are, then. And I couldn't be destroying any evidence, because any evidence remaining after the rod had been lying under running water and then bumping over sand would have to be more robust than bloodstains or fingerprints. I'm hardly going to do any harm winding the line in before it gets turned into crochet work.'

'I suppose that's true.' Johnson approached his nose to the rod. 'It doesn't tell me anything. What does the expert make of it?'

I stopped winding and examined the rod. 'Carbon fibre,' I said. 'Not top of the range but an expensive rod and not old – that model has only been on the market for about three years. It's seen some wear, but much of that may have been since it was dropped in the river. The owner lives locally or has rod-holders for his car.'

147

'How—?'

'The taped joints. They stop the joints twisting or coming apart in use, but the man who has to dismantle his rod to get it into the car doesn't usually bother. The reel's older but also very good. The line and backing look commonplace. In fact, I suspect that the whole lot could have been bought in our shop. Not "were", just "could have been". Except for the fly.' I finished reeling in and handed the rod to Johnson.

He stood studying the broken toy in his hands. 'Have you sold many of these rods?' he asked.

I was beginning to feel unhappy. 'Why do you care?' I retorted. 'If it couldn't have been Ken Berry's . . .'

'I'm interested. Do you have a magnifying glass with you?' We were getting very good at asking each other questions. This one, however, was more answerable. There is usually a magnifier in my kit. After 'spooning' a trout, a magnifying glass helps me to identify what the fish has been feeding on. I hunted it out and gave it to Johnson.

'Is your friend Mr Waterhouse back yet?' he asked.

'I saw his pick-up get back not very long ago. If he isn't at the house he'll be up at his release pen, brooding like a mother hen over his new poults. Why?'

Johnson looked apologetic. He blinked at me. His usually mild face was taking on a look of grim determination. 'Think of it this way,' he said. 'You fished up a rod. We know that a fisherman drowned, not long ago. Coincidence? Or is there some sort of a connection? I suppose the Colonel has a claim to the rod, but maybe it's evidence of some sort or another and the police ought to have it. Whichever you – we – hand it to, the other one could get uptight about it. We may as well eliminate any more innocent explanations before setting in motion a machine that we can't stop again. Otherwise we could end up looking a real pair of prats

148

and getting some people fed up at us who are just the sort of people we don't want to annoy.'

'That makes sense,' I admitted.

'That's right, it does. And I'll tell you why. How good a look did you take at the hooks?'

'Only to see that the barbs had been flattened,' I said. 'I was more interested in the dressing, which is definitely amateur.'

'Take a good look at the barbs. Hold the hooks by the shank and don't touch near the points.'

Johnson handed me the lens and I took the fly in my hand. Johnson was still holding the rod. 'Don't make any sudden movements,' I said, 'or you'll jag me.'

It took me a few seconds to make out what he wanted me to see. Caught between a hook and its flattened barb were two or three tiny fibres. I moved slightly to get them against a background of pale water and thought that they were probably green. 'Water weed,' I said. 'Or maybe a scrap of peacock herl from another fly.'

'Or green wool,' Johnson said flatly.

I resumed my seat on the rock and began bagging my rod and tackle. 'If so,' I said, 'what then?'

'Then we shall see. The ambulance driver commented how tatty Mr Berry's green sweater was. It was probably already well worn – nobody goes fishing in his best bib and tucker – and being rolled around in the river and then hauled over the rocks wouldn't have done it any favours. There would have been marks on the body, too, so I don't suppose that the pathologist would have paid attention to one particular scratch. How often have you fished this part of the river before today?'

It took my mind a few seconds to digest his first topic before turning to the second. 'Often,' I said. 'Not by courtesy of Ken Berry, nor of the Colonel. As far

149

as they were concerned I was a tradesman who ranked rather below a ghillie. But when the fishing was let to friends or clients of mine, I was often asked along.'

'All right, then. You know where Mr Berry drowned?'

I looked around vaguely. It came to me that I had only the vaguest idea. 'From what I was told, he went in somewhere around the top of the island. Presumably he drowned on the way down from there.'

Johnson nodded. 'He was pulled out about here,' he said, 'conveniently close to the drive. I saw photographs on the televisions just before my attack. They found his rod on the bank just about opposite the top end of the island where I was fishing, under those sycamores.'

'I know the place,' I said. 'There's a favourite lie for salmon near there.'

Johnson looked past me. When I looked round, Jim Waterhouse was approaching across the drive.

'So what's your question?' I asked.

'Later.'

We waited while the keeper crossed a stretch of rough grass and arrived at our rocky platform. I could tell that Jim was worried but he was not the man to worry passively. With him, worry called for an aggressive response. 'What's going on here?' he demanded.

Johnson was holding out the salmon rod. 'Mr James hooked this and hauled it out,' he said. 'No, don't touch it. Have you ever seen it before?'

'How the de'il would I ken that? One rod's much like another to me. I fish a bit mysel', but I'm no' a ghillie. If it was a gun, now...'

Friend or not, I couldn't let Jim get away with that. 'You're called on to act as a ghillie often enough,' I said gently.

He looked at me with reproach. 'Not by Mr Berry,' he said.

150

'Mr Berry's rod was found on the bank,' Johnson said. 'And there was no doubt about whose rod it was. His initials were burned into the cork handle.'

'I didno' mean that that might be Mr Berry's rod. Mr Berry asked guests along, whiles. If ane o' them dropped his rod in the water they'd likely not say, for fear of being laughed at.' He clamped his jaw shut.

Johnson glanced at me. 'How much would the rod be worth?'

'With reel and line? Around four hundred or so.'

Johnson nodded. 'I see. Is the Colonel at home?' he asked Jim.

'Aye. He'll be down here soon enough. I was away up at my release pen, so the wife phoned him when she saw that you'd strayed to the main stream and were getting a' steamed up over some damned old rod out o' the water.'

'I wonder why she was so concerned,' Johnson said. 'This rod's not so old. This model's only – what, Wallace?'

'About three years old,' I said. Jim shot me another reproachful glance. I decided that if he was going to blame me for Johnson's questions I might as well ask a few of my own. 'Does the Colonel dress his own salmon flies?' I asked him.

Jim shook his head vehemently. 'Never,' he said.

'Would you recognize his rod?'

'Aye. And that's no' it.'

'What make of rod does he use for salmon?' I persisted.

'A fifteen-foot Hexagraph.'

Johnson was frowning at the irrelevance but I might have persisted with my questions except that a smartly painted and polished Isuzu Trooper pulled up in the drive with a squeal of rubber. I saw a brief argument between the two occupants before Colonel McInsch quitted the driver's seat and came stamping down to the river. He was dressed in the tweedy way that passes for smart in the country but a bulge in his jacket gave him a lopsided appearance.

The Colonel was not in the best of moods and he chose to focus his glare on me. 'Waterhouse was to let you fish for trout. You've been after my salmon. You're nothing but a damned poacher!'

Telling myself to stay calm for the sake of my heart, I opened my creel and exhibited my catch of brown trout. 'You're welcome to look at my gear,' I said. 'If you think I go after salmon with a nine-foot trout rod and not a hook with me bigger than a Ten, you'll believe in Santa.'

The Colonel pointed indignantly at the rod in Johnson's hands. 'What about that, then?'

'Mr James was fishing for trout but he caught a salmon – Johnson paused mischievously – 'rod. This one. Do you recognize it?'

'No. And I'd like to know what authority you have, to interrogate me in front of my staff and . . . and guest.'

Apparently I was a guest now, all of a sudden.

'Am I interrogating you?' Johnson asked. He was rather white around the gills, but determined. 'We'd just pulled a rod out of the river, which seemed a bit of a coincidence so soon after the drowning of your neighbour. Surely it's only logical to ask if you recognized it?'

'Well, I don't.' The Colonel held out his hand. 'Give me the rod,' he said. 'I'll deal with it.'

I saw Johnson's grip on the rod tighten and he backed away a pace. 'In the normal course of events,' he said stiffly, 'I'd hand the rod over to you or your staff, but in view of Mr Berry's death I feel obliged to ask a few questions, looking for an innocent explanation for the presence of this rod in the river, before handing over the rod.' He paused, swallowed and moistened his lips. I thought that he was showing a great deal of courage for a usually timid man. 'If you prefer not to answer questions in this informal setting, then perhaps I should hand the rod over to the police. No doubt they'll deliver the rod to you in the end, but they may have a few questions of their own to ask first.'

NINE

Colonel McInsch stood for several long moments, out-wardly impassive although I sensed that inwardly he was seething. I was slightly apart from the others and I was the only one sitting down, yet his eyes wandered my way and he seemed to be particularly aware of me. I thought, without knowing quite why I thought it, that I was the reason for his hesitation.

With an effort, the Colonel brought himself under control. 'Perhaps I'm being unreasonable,' he said at last. 'No, I don't recognize that rod and, frankly, I'm not terribly interested. Such things can travel far enough. It may have been dropped in miles upstream and come down on the spate. If it had been dropped in near here, I'd have heard about it.'

I saw Johnson looking at me out of the corner of his eye and I gave a tiny headshake. A rod with line and hook trailing is not an ideal shape for travelling with the current, over shingle and especially through weed.

'Leaving that aside for the moment,' Johnson said, 'I take it you agree that the dredging up of a salmon rod so soon after the drowning of a salmon fisherman is enough of a coincidence to require explanation.'

'Frankly, I think you're making a mountain out of a molehill,' said the Colonel. 'The rod can't have belonged to Berry. His rod was found on the bank. And at a damned easy place to slip in. Yes?'

'True, I suppose.' Johnson turned to me. 'Wal, you know where Mr Berry's rod was found.'

'And yes,' I said. 'The Colonel's right. If your over-head back-cast isn't going to get caught up in the trees, there's only one good place. It's too deep to wade out and some reeds make Spey or roll casting difficult. You have to get out to the brink where there's a flat and rather slippery rock. Toppling in would be . . . as easy as falling off a rock.' The Colonel gave a grunt of agreement. Rashly, I decided to give him a little more support. 'These rods are quite common. Colonel McInsch bought another very similar rod in the shop just a few days after the accident. But Mr Berry's was quite different. I sold him that one too.'

The Colonel flinched and I knew that I had said what was, from his point of view, the wrong thing. In my muddled thinking I had only meant to confirm that the rod I had just recovered had not belonged to the late Mr Berry, but I had drawn attention to another coincidence, if not a direct connection between the rod and the Colonel. Presumably this explained his reluctance to speak out in front of me. And he had decided to be frank only because he had no idea that even while I was confined to my chair in the window above the shop all the receipts and invoices had passed through my hands.

'If it was easy to slip and fall in,' Johnson said dog-gedly, 'it would be equally easy to be pushed or pulled in. There are some tiny green fibres caught under the flattened barb of one of the hooks. I think that it's my duty to call them to the attention of the police. The Forensic boffins will be able to state whether they came from the green sweater Mr Berry was wearing.'

Colonel McInsch closed his eyes for a few seconds. 'No need for all that fiddle-faddle,' he said at last. 'I'll tell you exactly what happened – in a little more detail

155

than I found it necessary to give the sheriff, in view of the fact that the enquiry was into a perfectly simple accident.'

'Go on,' Johnson said.

The Colonel gathered up his thoughts. He spoke with precision. In his mind, I thought that he was giving his evidence afresh before the sheriff. 'I had just cast across the river, to a favourite lie near the far bank. But it was chilly weather, not unlike today's, and any fish would have been lying deep, so I was using a fast-sinking line. My hooks had caught up on the bottom. That's when Ken Berry chose to arrive on the far bank. He flew off the handle straight away, as he had a habit of doing.'

Johnson looked puzzled.

'It's considered perfectly fair to cast across the river to beneath the opposite bank,' I explained, 'except when there's somebody fishing from that bank.'

The Colonel nodded approvingly. 'I'd made my cast before I saw him coming and by the time I'd freed my line he'd started a shouting match. My behaviour was perfectly in order, but the blasted man wouldn't listen to reason. He got more and more agitated. Next thing I knew, he'd lost his footing on the slippery rock, dropped his rod and fallen in.

'He was a non-swimmer and so'm I. I was just about to run for help when my rod, which I'd laid down in the grass while we shouted at each other, suddenly shot into the water. Either he'd fouled my line on the way by or he'd clutched it like the proverbial straw. I'm sure you can see why I didn't want to ... to muddy the waters by bringing all this out in front of the sheriff. The papers can make up a scandal out of nothing. It would be my guess that that's how any fibres of wool got under the barbs.'

The Colonel paused. I could see that his brain was in

overdrive with an effort either of memory or invention, quite probably both. 'It came to me that the current often brings flotsam ashore here and that even if he didn't manage to struggle ashore here himself, if he was still trailing my rod the rod might be within reach, so I sprinted down here or' – he smiled a twisted smile – 'as near to a sprint as I can get these days. As it happened, my stepson was fishing at this end of the island. I sent him to phone and while he was absent Ken Berry drifted within reach. The rod had vanished altogether. Presumably my crimped barbs had let the hook drop out. I did what I could for him but it was too late. And that's absolutely all that I have to say on the matter. The subject is closed.'

The Colonel nodded with finality and turned away.

As the local MP the Colonel carried a lot of weight and if Johnson pushed any further he could be putting his job on the line. Hoping against hope that the bulge under the Colonel's jacket was his mobile phone and not a handgun, I decided to pick up the ball. 'It's a good story,' I said to Johnson. 'It could almost be true. Not quite, but almost.'

That did it. The Colonel turned on his heel so quickly that he almost screwed himself into the ground. 'What the hell is that supposed to mean?' he barked in a voice that had usually been reserved for the parade ground or for hecklers in the Commons.

'Just what I said,' I told him. 'Like any other politician, you can give a good answer off the cuff, but there are flaws which let you down. For one thing, that isn't your rod. You use a Hexagraph. I remember now that I ordered it for you. You spoke to my wife about it but I placed the order.'

The subject, it seemed, was not as closed as all that. I expected him to explain that a man can have more than one rod, which would have then involved me in a lengthy explanation of how I came to know that he did not. But he decided to take a different line. 'When I say "my rod", the Colonel explained coldly, 'I'm using the term loosely, as any angler would if he was referring to the rod that he had in his hand at the time. In point of fact, it had been rather a spur-of-the-moment decision to fish at all, because I had taken a stroll down this way and seen fish moving for the first time since Parliament went into recess.'

'You said that the fish were lying deep,' I reminded him.

'Fish on the move can come up,' he retorted. 'Rather than walk all the way home, I borrowed . . .' the Colonel's voice died away while he gave frantic thought and then came back strongly '. . . I called at Jim Waterhouse's cottage and borrowed his rod.'

'And his waders?' Johnson asked. 'The ambulance driver said that you were wearing chest waders.'

'And chest waders,' the Colonel said quickly. 'After losing his rod for him like that, I bought Waterhouse another one. I felt that it was the least I could do. Isn't that so?'

His question was aimed at Jim, who had been standing by with a frozen expression, silent and half forgotten. I saw Jim's eyebrows go up, but he nodded. Paradoxically, my respect for the Colonel went up. He must be an exceptionally good employer to inspire such unquestioning trust.

'I presume that you're satisfied now,' the Colonel snapped at me. 'You can go, Waterhouse,' he added.

Rather than put Jim on the spot I waited until he was out of earshot. 'I'm afraid not,' I said. 'Jim's still using the rod I got for him five years ago. I know it's the same one, because I got him a bargain of a rod that had been damaged in transit and I recognized it in his house this morning. I could still see the repair I did to

158

it. What's more, I could make a damned good guess as to who dressed that fly, and it wasn't Jim Waterhouse. He never ties his own flies.'

'And no more do I.'

'I know that.'

The Colonel was outwardly impassive. To an opponent across the floor of the House he would have seemed still to be in full command of himself, but from close to I could see a tremor in his hand and some beads of sweat that could not be explained by the cool of the day. Johnson read the signs and regained strength. 'You might also care to explain why you sent your stepson to call the emergency services,' he said. 'The ambulance driver said that you made the emergency call on your own portable phone, the one bulging under your jacket.'

Colonel Ivor McInsch MP drew himself up and up until his feet seemed ready to leave the ground, but this time his hesitation became a silence. If he could not think faster in the face of the enemy, I thought, it was no wonder that his military career had stalled short of general rank. And he would never make it to the premiership.

'I can't let you do this,' said a new voice. Nick Lamontine had left the car and approached us. I had noticed him earlier, listening unobtrusively and from a distance. Now he came up beside his stepfather.

'Be quiet, you young fool,' the Colonel snapped. 'If you have it in mind to ... to fabricate some tale in order to whitewash me, you're going to do more harm than good.'

The younger man laughed without the least trace of amusement. 'It's too late', he said. 'Too many contradictions are beginning to show. Don't think that I don't appreciate what you've done and what you were trying to do. All things being equal I'd have let you get on

159

with it. But even Mother wouldn't have expected you to lay so much on the line.' If his speech was gracious, his tone was not. He managed to make the words sound patronizing. In the Colonel's shoes I would have used them to give him a kick up the backside, but the Colonel still had himself in hand.

Lamontine turned to Johnson. 'As you and Mr James seem to have guessed between you, it was exactly the other way round. I was fishing up at the head of Island Pool and I had the slanging match with the unpleasant Mr Berry. When he slipped and fell in I ran and asked Mrs Waterhouse to phone for help and an ambulance, but my stepfather was fishing down here. The current brought the body almost to his feet. Not knowing that I had gone to phone, he used his mobile and his message got through before mine. Then he did what he could. But it was too late.' He paused and seemed to make a conscious effort, only partly successful, to put on a conciliatory expression. 'Remember,' he said, 'no real harm has been done. I can only ask you to be generous.'

Johnson's eyes switched from him to the Colonel. 'So why the fabrication? Why tell it the other way round to the sheriff, and on oath? Why lay yourself open to a charge of perjury, to be followed by political ruin?'

'I didn't want the boy mixed up in it,' the Colonel said gruffly. 'I still don't. He's all that I have left of his mother, you see.'

'I suggest,' Johnson said to me, 'that Colonel McInsch may have felt that if the truth should begin to emerge, as a Member of Parliament he would stand a better chance than his stepson would before a jury of ordinary, disbelieving mortals like ourselves.'

The Colonel turned white. 'That suggestion is slanderous and I resent it deeply. I shall be consulting my solicitor with a view to taking action. And I have nothing further to say at this time. Give me that rod.' He moved forward purposefully.

I stood up quickly and put myself between the Colonel and Johnson. 'Nobody has been forcing you to say a word,' I pointed out. 'If what truth should start to emerge?' I asked Johnson.

By way of a partial answer, Johnson pointed to the lead weight which was half hidden by the feathers of the big salmon fly. 'An Arlesey bomb,' he said. 'That's sea-fishing tackle, unheard-of for salmon fishing. But if you happened to have one in your tackle bag it wouldn't take a second to clip on.

'You know better than I do, Wal, that when you're fly-casting you only have the weight of the line itself to carry it out. Up there, with the trees behind, you'd have a hell of a job casting a fly over somebody on the far bank; I wasn't getting beyond about halfway, when I didn't get caught up in the trees behind me. But you could easily clip on a weight which would make it perform like casting a spinner, needing no back cast at all. You could easily cast over a man on the opposite bank. If he was on a slippery footing, one good pull would do it. Once he was in the water, if he was still hooked or hanging on to your line, it would only be necessary to let go of the rod.'

'And,' I said, 'we may find that Mr Lamontine had a strong motivation for desiring Ken Berry's death. The Colonel, quixotically, decided to keep him out of the limelight. That's why he sent him away from the scene.'

'What motivation?' the Colonel roared. 'We never liked the man and I've made no secret of the fact, but I defy you to produce any motive that either of us might have had for killing him. I am not going to stay here and be insulted.'

Again he turned away, but Nick Lamontine still faced

us. His eyes were narrowed and there was something intimidating about the set of his head on his shoulders. It seemed to me that we had already said too much.

'I think that we should let the Colonel go on his way,' I said.

Either Johnson did not read the danger signs or he was too carried away to be warned. 'But we'll hang onto the rod,' he said. 'Between us, I'm sure that we can work out the motivations and point the police in the direction of some very useful witnesses.'

The Colonel stopped as though he had walked into a wall and span round. 'I'm saying no more, but if you're going to dream up another host of wild theories you're not doing it behind my back.'

The two men had us backed against the slight drop to the flowing water and their mood was unstable. Lamontine was ripe for explosion and I guessed that Colonel McInsch, having already forgiven the first betrayal, would move heaven and earth to protect his late wife's son.

But they were facing the river while I was facing the land and between the trees I had glimpsed a car moving along the drive. It had come from the direction of the road and had vanished behind the nearest trees. Any sound that it made was covered by the hiss and gurgle of the river. Visitors for the Colonel would surely have driven on, reappearing. If this was our lift, there would at least be witnesses and somebody to go for help; and if it was Keith, I had a sublime faith that, as always, he would know what to do. For the moment, it seemed important to hold their attention, to delay any drastic action until the situation resolved itself.

I said, 'Two men tried to saddle Jim Waterhouse with a false charge of poisoning raptors. The Colonel decided to fight fire with fire and the two of you gave Jim an alibi. So far so good. Many of us who suspected the validity of the alibi have been laughing and saying that we would have done the same.

'But somebody, and I think I can guess who, had seen the two of you fishing this bit of river on at least two occasions that day and Jim wasn't with you. They ran to Ken Berry. Mr Berry tackled the Colonel and they had an argument on the garage forecourt.

'Instead of running to the police, Mr Berry decided to twist the knife the other way. He tipped off a reporter of his acquaintance, Sid Jubilee.'

Nick Lamontine made a sudden movement but the Colonel put out a hand and checked him. 'Wait,' he said. 'I want to hear this.'

The pressure was building up. The more time it had to build the more violently it would blow. But I had seen a figure among the trees, less than fifty yards away.

'Instead of publishing the story, Jubilee decided to resort to an oblique form of blackmail,' I said. I could hear my own voice and it was becoming higher and quicker as the confrontation became more ominous. Johnson and I were not in fighting condition. 'Mr Berry expected quick results in the form of publication. He didn't know that Jubilee was darting around, getting statements from anybody who was prepared to talk, and he got frustrated. Across the river, he shouted some threat about reporting both of you to the police for perjury. So Nick clipped a weight onto his line and pulled him in.

'Jubilee found that Ralph Enterkin was a tough negotiator. He wasn't going to get out of it as much as he'd hoped and there may have been a threat that if he pushed it any further there would be awful retribution. The law has been known to deal harshly with blackmailers and yet keep the victim's name out of the media. Jubilee decided that he might be able to get two smaller bites out of the same cherry. He put pressure on Nick, through Nick's ladyfriend, to listen in on phonecalls. And so he learned that the money was liable to be carried, by the hand of an elderly solicitor, from the bank to the solicitor's office. Jubilee brought in a couple of toughs to intercept the money, knowing that if it was stolen before it reached him he could repeat the blackmail attempt.' I hesitated and decided, if possible, to drive a wedge between the Colonel and his stepson. 'How much of a cut were you going to get, Nick?' I asked him.

Nick flared up on the instant. 'That does it!' he growled. He stiffened. His attitude reminded me of nothing so much as some animal, crouched and ready to spring.

The Colonel put out a hand. 'Hold on,' he said. 'I want to hear the rest of it. Always know the strength of the enemy.'

Nick steadied without relaxing. His eyes switched between mine and Johnson's with angry movements like the tail of a wildcat. 'We know it,' he said grimly. 'If they run to the police with that story, the police only have to seek out the witnesses and they've got the lot. I get sent down, and if you don't follow me into prison you end up in disgrace. Neither of us wants that!'

'What are you trying to suggest?' Colonel McInsch looked nervously round but nobody was in sight. I began to wonder whether I had been wrong. An ache began in my chest and left arm.

'One good push,' Lamontine said. There was saliva on his chin and the light of madness in his eye. 'It's no worse than what I've already done. They're both heart patients. If they fight, they probably die anyway. If they don't they drown. We have a good story. One of them slipped and fell in, the other tried to save him. I saw the whole thing even if you want to stay out of it. And after that ... they've practically told us who the witnesses are.'

The Colonel was holding Nick's arm. 'But I want to know—'

'Know nothing,' Nick said roughly. 'Let's get it over before somebody comes along. I've heard enough.'

'And so have I,' said a new voice. Ian Fellowes in plain clothes came out from behind a small clump of holly and walked towards us. He stopped in front of the Colonel. 'You know who I am?'

'You're that police inspector who married Calder's daughter,' the Colonel said dully. 'You asked me a few questions after Ken Berry was drowned.'

'I shall be asking some more. I am taking you both into custody.'

'On what charge? I hope you know what you're doing, young man,' the Colonel said grimly.

Ian smiled. 'No, you don't. You're hoping against hope that I don't know what I'm doing. The charge for the moment is threatening behaviour but more serious charges will follow.'

Colonel McInsch still had his courage. 'If you had eavesdropped for a minute longer,' he said, 'you would have heard me refuse to allow any violence.'

'I hope that that's true,' Ian said. 'But the decision will be up to a court. No, don't say a word.' As if by prestidigitation, he produced a pair of handcuffs. 'Please put out your right hands.' Lamontine, I could see, was preparing to run or to make a fight of it. 'And don't do anything foolish,' Ian continued. 'I have men all around.'

We all looked. From time to time, a figure in uniform could be glimpsed among the trees. If never more than one at a time was in sight and they all looked surprisingly like Detective Constable Fraser, Ian's usual driver whenever he needed such a refinement, I had more sense than to say so.

The Colonel sighed. 'Very well,' he said. 'We can soon sort this out.'

Lamontine looked as though he was still thinking of attacking Johnson and me and damn the consequences, but thought better of it. 'This is a set-up,' he said. 'It has to be. How do you like being an *agent provocateur*?' he asked me.

I shook my head.

Each man, as ordered, held out a wrist. 'No,' Ian said. 'The right wrist, both of you.' He called out to DC Fraser.

As the two men were led away, stumbling awkwardly, he added, 'Doing it that way makes it much more difficult for them to take to their heels. Fraser can give them the warning about their rights. He enjoys that sort of thing whereas I always feel a prat using one or other of the same old clichés. Are you two all right for the moment?' he asked anxiously. 'I'm going to have to radio for another car. I can't transport you alongside those two. There's always hell to pay if blood gets spilled inside a police car.'

When I came to think about it, the warning signs of angina had vanished but I took a squirt of Nitrolingual as a precaution. 'I'm fine,' I said.

Johnson nodded. 'What put you on their track?' he asked. 'You arrived in the nick of time.'

'I wasn't on their track at all,' Ian said. We had to wait while he produced his personal radio and requested the dispatch of a back-up car. 'When I saw you silhouetted against the water,' he resumed, 'there was something menacing about two of the figures and the other two – you two, I could recognize you – looked defensive and vulnerable. I thought that you were probably only having an argument about where you ought to be fishing but I thought I'd make a discreet approach, just in case. And when I got within earshot, they were discussing whether to kill you both. So I doubled back and told Fraser to do his impression of a small army while I prepared to leap to your aid.'

'Then why are you here?' I asked.

'I'm here because Janet and my mother-in-law have gone to Kelso leaving Keith stuck in the shop. And Deborah doesn't have the use of a car until mine comes back from the repairer. If then,' Ian added grimly. 'So Keith phoned me to come and pick you up. As it happened, when the message reached me I was on the way back from delivering a suspect to Edinburgh, so I could manage it.' We looked at him blankly. 'I'm your lift,' he explained patiently.

TEN

It was midwinter before Nick Lamontine came to trial
and near the end of a shooting season which I had
enjoyed more than ever before, in part because just to
be alive at all was a bonus but also because I was
spared all the stumbling over difficult ground which,
on all but the most upmarket shoots, can take the fine
edge off the best of days. I still had to be careful,
especially in the colder weather, but my angina was
little more than a memory. All the same, I had no
objection to being Land Rovered tenderly from one
drive to the next and allowed to be a perpetual standing
Gun instead of having to take my turn as a beater or
walking Gun, forcing my way through spruce plan-
tations with needles going down my neck or, worse,
floundering through gorse or long heather. A heart
condition is not all bad news.

Sitting in Edinburgh, the High Court had already
sent the two hard men away. Mention was made of a
woman accomplice but Mrs Ritson-Jones had not figured on the security videos which had so thoroughly
convicted the two men and for lack of any other evidence she was not charged. When Nick Lamontine
came up the court was sitting in Newton Lauder, so
that although my evidence had been given some days
earlier, I managed to get back into court to hear the
verdict.

If Nick Lamontine had come up before a fishing judge, things might have been different. But defence counsel – whom I had taught to fish some years earlier – forced me to modify some of my evidence and later produced several carefully selected experts (so-called) who were prepared to suggest explanations as to why a salmon fisher might innocently attach an Arlesey bomb to his fly. Not one of them made sense to me, especially in the context of a river nowhere more than sixteen feet deep, but the jury must have accepted that there was reasonable doubt. The remainder of the evidence might be suggestive but it was not quite damning. After a prolonged withdrawal, they brought in a verdict of *not proven*. Nick Lamontine was free.

It had been decided that no legal action would be taken against the Colonel, but he was disgraced and his career in tatters. He had been forced to resign his seat in Parliament and this was to be the subject of an imminent by-election. Normally one would have expected the heir to Castle Berry to be elected as a matter of course, but so many other contenders had arrived to split the vote that there seemed to be a high probability that Screaming Lord Sutch would be our next parliamentary representative. As Keith among others said, Sutch was no dafter than the rest.

On the day after the verdict, I was alone in the shop when the Colonel walked in. I had not seen him except in the distance since our confrontation beside the river and I was not sure what attitude to take. I was reasonably sure that he would not resort to violence. More pressing was the question of whether Nick Lamontine was with him and after my blood.

The Colonel saw me looking past him and smiled grimly. 'My stepson's leaving for Australia,' he said. He glanced at his watch. 'In fact, I suppose he's airborne by now. I'll take a dozen boxes of Eley Grand Prix,' he added without any change of tone. 'Number Six shot. We're running short.'

I took his cartridges off the shelf and stacked them. The Colonel leaned his elbows on the glass counter. 'I was sure he'd get off,' he said. 'In fact, I thought they were going to bring in *not guilty*. But I also knew that he was finished in this country. He has an uncle, his mother's brother, with a sheep-farm in Australia and he's going out there to work. They'll knock the stuffing out of him, or into him, whichever way you want to look at it. I'll take one of those.' He put his finger on the glass above a leather cartridge bag. I had a feeling that I was being offered an apology and a reassurance.

'All that he really did wrong, up to that last day,' I said, picking my words, 'was to lose his rag when a singularly nasty man threatened him. All the same, I'm just as happy that he'll be as far away from me as he can possibly get.'

'I'm glad that you understand,' he said. And with an apparent change of subject: 'I wouldn't want to be in the shoes of that journalist.'

'Nor I,' I said. As the facts had reached the light of day, Sid Jubilee had been savaged by his colleagues of the press. His attempt to extort blackmail had been adjudged to be no more than attempted corruption, quite normal among the gentlemen of the press, while his conspiracy with the thugs had never been proved; but it was certain that he would never work again in Britain. I had been surprised to discover that there was a line below which a journalist may never sink.

The Colonel looked directly at me for the first time and there was a great sadness in his eyes. 'I wasn't going to help him against you, you know.'

'I know,' I said. 'But if he'd gone for me . . .'

'Which side would I have fought on? Would I have opposed him physically?' He sighed and then shrugged, suddenly looking another ten years older. 'I don't know and I'm glad I didn't have to find out. I might not have had the guts, let alone the heart.'

He saw me blink at the last word and he produced a smile of surprising warmth. 'As I said before, he was all that I had left of my wife. Well,' he straightened up and spoke briskly, 'the salmon will be coming back into season soon and I could use a new sink-tip double-taper line. Don't keep me standing here all day.'

	DATE DUE		